DEAR HEARTS

STORIES

BARBARA MILLER BILES

*Best Wishes
Barbara Biles
October 2, 2020*

inanna poetry & fiction series

INANNA PUBLICATIONS AND EDUCATION INC.
TORONTO, CANADA

Copyright © 2020 Barbara Miller Biles

Except for the use of short passages for review purposes, no part of this book may be reproduced, in part or in whole, or transmitted in any form or by any means, electronically or mechanically, including photocopying, recording, or any information or storage retrieval system, without prior permission in writing from the publisher or a licence from the Canadian Copyright Collective Agency (Access Copyright).

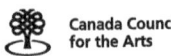 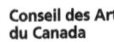  

We gratefully acknowledge the support of the Canada Council for the Arts and the Ontario Arts Council for our publishing program. We also acknowledge the financial support of the Government of Canada.

Cover design: Val Fullard

Library and Archives Canada Cataloguing in Publication

Title: Dear hearts : stories / Barbara Miller Biles.
Names: Biles, Barbara Miller, 1946– author.
Series: Inanna poetry & fiction series.
Description: Series statement: Inanna poetry & fiction series
Identifiers: Canadiana (print) 20200208233 | Canadiana (ebook) 20200208268 | ISBN 9781771337533 (softcover) | ISBN 9781771337540 (epub) | ISBN 9781771337557 (Kindle) | ISBN 9781771337564 (pdf)
Classification: LCC PS8603.I55 D42 2020 | DDC C813/.6—dc23

Printed and bound in Canada
Inanna Publications and Education Inc.
210 Founders College, York University
4700 Keele Street, Toronto, Ontario M3J 1P3 Canada
Telephone: (416) 736-5356 Fax (416) 736-5765
Email: inanna.publications@inanna.ca Website: www.inanna.ca

For my Dearest Hearts,

Alison, Stephen, William and Mae.

Table of Contents

TENDER HEARTS

Lila

3

Silvia

7

Gourmet Cooking

11

No Regrets

18

Svea

20

Rosemary

29

Snipe Hunting

41

GENEVA STORIES

Rockin' Around The Royal Bank of Canada
53

Here's Looking At You
62

The Case
72

Gone
81

Vive la Révolution
90

Marrying Stationery
101

SURREAL HEARTS

Transforming Doctor Zhivago
109

Shifting
115

TABLE OF CONTENTS

Flight 2100
123

Smile
129

Saving Britannica
138

Special Occasions
148

JANET STORIES

Life in Cars
157

Police and Matisse
164

Hair Matters
173

Jumping to Conclusions
177

SORRY HEARTS

Fee Fine
187

The Guardian
195

Burnt Sienna
200

Tattoos
205

Acknowledgements
214

TENDER HEARTS

Lila

❋

If you want to know about Lila as a child, look at the painting called *The Two Sisters (On The Terrace)*, oil on canvas, by Pierre-Auguste Renoir in 1881. Apparently they weren't really sisters, but that's beside the point. Like the younger girl, Lila was a delicate-looking child, but with flaxen hair and intense blue eyes. In Renoir's painting the youngest is wearing a royal blue hat decorated with fresh garden flowers. This reminds me of Lila in two ways: first, picking crocuses along the railway tracks and then sitting in the grass, weaving crocuses and dandelions into necklaces or bracelets or coronets for our hair, her with graceful fingers, me with fumbling hands. And I think of the spray of pink carnations on her sister Iris's casket and the vision of Lila ripping away a handful of the flowers and holding them to her breast.

We were only ten, and we were fascinated with the life of Lila's teenage sister Iris. She had the same delicate features as Lila, but there was something steely about Iris and somehow that made the boys even more determined to capture her affection. Renoir's older sister is wearing a scarlet hat and a corsage, front and centre, on her coat. She is beautiful, like an angel, with rosy lips and wide brows. Her eyes look off to the side as though she is remembering something warm and precious. At least that's my impression. (Pardon the allusion.) This reminds me of Iris listening to and singing "Earth Angel" along with The Crew Cuts, over and over.

Lila and I mouthed the words to the song in her bedroom, which was next door to Iris's. Lila did the melody and I did the doo-wop. We would stand on her bed, holding imaginary mics and at times knocking each other over and collapsing into giggles. We imagined that Iris was singing to Ronny Wilson, even though he wasn't there.

Ronny Wilson drove by regularly on summer nights in his father's Oldsmobile, and if Iris happened to be outside or even looking outside he would stop and honk and take her for a ride around town. Maybe even go for a pop at Shakey's. Ronny was a serious boy, track-star muscular, with dark eyes and Brylcreemed hair. He planned to be a mechanic like his father and eventually take over Wilson Motors. He had eyes only for Iris, and Lila and I mooned over that fact. In retrospect his commitment seems a bit boring. Where was the game in it all? Perhaps Iris felt the same after Darryl Sexton came to town.

Darryl came, just for the summer, to work with his Uncle Mel and Aunt Mary in their novelty shop since Mary was now preoccupied with a new baby girl. At first Darryl helped stock the shelves with bolts of cloth, kitchen towels, colouring books and crayons, yo-yos, cheap trinkets, and wind-up toys. The Sextons were all pretty new to town and were themselves a novelty, especially Darryl. Mel's Variety Store soon became a hangout for teenagers, especially giggling girls. Darryl was a magnet: hip, brash, and good looking. Then he switched to a job at the cemetery, which only enhanced his aura: he sported a dark tan and sun-bleached hair from the hours spent cutting grass and digging graves, shirtless and without a cap. We didn't know why he changed jobs, and the Sextons wouldn't say. Maybe he missed the outdoors.

Lila and I continued to believe that Iris had gone to the cemetery to visit their grandmother's grave because her mother said it was so. Ronny Wilson liked this version as well. At least that's what he said. It wasn't until Lila and I became teenagers ourselves that we realized the place had a dual purpose: it was a resting place for dead bodies and a make-out place for the town's teenagers. On the day she died, Iris rode her bike out there all on her own rather than with her usual group of friends. And Darryl Sexton drove her back with a gash in the back of her head, blood matting her hair and drool on her cherry lips. He said she slipped and fell back on her grandmother's headstone. My dad went back to the cemetery to retrieve her bike for the family and I heard him say that it was nowhere near her grandmother's grave. My mother told him to shush.

I think Ronny and Lila developed a bond right then and there, but it wasn't until she turned sixteen and he was working for his dad that they considered romance. (But we didn't use the word romance then.) They started to go together, riding around in the Oldsmobile, necking at the cemetery, listening to Bobby Darin and Connie Francis, and dancing to Buddy Holly and Chuck Berry covers at Regents' dances. The song that really held them together though was "Teen Angel."

They always turned up the volume and sang full volume. I wondered how Lila felt about the "own true love" part and the possibility of being a stand-in for Iris.

Lila was one of the first girls to join Ronny and his friends in the popular teen pastime of drinking and smoking in cars. She acted as if this got her into some exclusive club. I stayed out of it for the most part, but I did always go along for the ride. For Ronny it was just a phase. For Lila it was different; she saw it as a sign of sophistication and belonging that continued on past the car-riding stage. "Do you mind if I smoke?" she would say after she had already lit up.

These days people really do mind and aren't afraid to say so, and Lila has to lean or mostly sit outside, since her balance is unreliable—with her left eyelid drooping and her tongue searching hard for the filter. Her breathing can get pretty heavy at times. When he can, Ronny will even carry her from one place to another, especially after she has had her bottle of wine. Now he drives her to the cemetery, whereas before she preferred to visit Iris during the daytime, all on her own, while Ronny worked at the garage. Ronny is one of those rare men who remain devoted to their wives no matter what.

Darryl Sexton never left town and several wives were said to enjoy his homemade wine at one time or another. It would be the ultimate betrayal if Lila became one of them.

Unlike Edgar Degas (another Impressionist), Renoir avoided the darker side of life in his paintings, but there is one portrait from 1876 called *Head of a Woman* that makes me think of Lila now. The woman has dark hair and brown eyes, unlike Lila, but they share that delicate look, with sad eyes and pale skin blending into an off-white dress. Everything below the eyes and in the background becomes vague and diffuse. The background has been painted using the colours of a faded field of crocuses, and the woman's face is like a dandelion going to seed.

Silvia

❂

HER HAIR WAS BLONDE AS A CHILD, then it went prematurely grey. Everyone thought of her as ash-blonde—beautiful but mature. In spite of her resolve to become a biologist she fell into the same trap as dozens of other girls in the sixties, believing in the whole amusing idea of free love: equal opportunity to hop in the sack with no repercussions. So funny I forgot to laugh.

Silvia got pregnant the first time out, and like her namesake, Rhea Silvia—who was seduced in the forest by the god Mars to become the mother of Romulus and Remus—she bore twins. That was the end of her own concocted tale of perpetual virginity. In Silvia's case the seduction was in the back of a Chevy Nova at the edge of Groat Ravine. She had the choice to either end the resulting pregnancy or put her boys up for adoption. Unlike Rhea Silvia, whose boys were set adrift on the Tiber River and then rescued and suckled by the she-wolf Lupa, Silvia chose to stay with her Aunt Margaret in Toronto for a stint and from then on wondered what kind of life her boys would lead. Certainly not likely to create a city like Rome or commit fratricide.

You might consider me lucky by contrast. My first time was in a motel after the Wauneita Ball. It had all been arranged ahead of time unbeknownst to me. You must know that for a girl of the sixties, in spite of the liberation, sex was shocking the first time, as in *Am I really doing this?* There was less worry about contracting a venereal disease since we all believed that it couldn't actually happen to nice girls—and AIDS was not yet around. But pregnancy, that was always possible.

In spite of the risk, I took no responsibility regarding prevention because it wouldn't have been proper to anticipate sex. When I returned to Kelsey Hall that night I realized I still had a safe stuck inside me, filled with all the semen needed to create a child. My explanation to myself was that yes, I must be in love. So much for the free love part. Why was I lucky? No pregnancy, either the first time out or any time after.

Silvia confessed to me, once she was back in Edmonton, that she delivered and gave away her babies, and that Marty Weston was the father though he was unaware of it. Marty was a law student, destined to become Chief Judge Weston. The twins eventually found them both through Parent Finders, which was a relief and a heart stopper to Silvia and must have been a shocker to Marty.

Some claim that Rhea Silvia, instead of being seduced by Mars, was really impregnated by the demi-god Hercules, who was himself illegitimate, or even by her uncle Amulius, who had first forced her to become a Vestal Virgin so he could keep the throne of Alba Longa free of her descendants. Similarly, Marty, feeling vulnerable in his venerable position, suggested that any number of others could be the father of Silvia's twin boys. But I knew Silvia. She was traumatized by the immediate pregnancy and had not been with any other guy for more than a year after their bout in the Chevy. And DNA proved Marty's paternity. Now how does one prove one is the son of a god?

I ran into Marty once while riding an escalator at The Bay. This was before the twins had tracked him down. He commented on how young I looked. Still pretty, he said. I have a compact figure, having had no kids to stretch my stomach out of shape, and unlike Silvia I have very few grey hairs. On the other hand Marty had developed quite a belly, and his once-curly hair had receded and flattened considerably. I didn't mention Silvia's secret.

The twins, Troy and Hardy, are fraternal, so you are not tempted to treat them as if they are the same, whether in brain, heart, or soul. They call me Auntie as I have stuck by Silvia through thick and thin (unlike her husband). I was there for her first meeting with the boys, and I am happy to be in their lives as I have no children of my own. They were raised in a congenial family of market gardeners in Simcoe County. Troy Dobson, tall and prematurely grey like his mother, took his childhood experiences to the Ontario Agricultural College in Guelph and became an expert in organic and small-scale agronomy and the marketing of fair trade agricultural products for profit in third world countries. Through his travels he met and became the husband of Luisa, a Bolivian beauty, and they in turn named their daughter Silvia.

This was before Troy found his mother. Maybe he knew about her long before he contacted her. But still, talk about coincidence.

Hardy Dobson, who looks a lot like Marty and shares many of his traits, including a large belly, has his own law practice in Barrie, specializing in international adoptions and custody battles. He has yet to get married, though he has two girls. He says he is on excellent terms with their mother.

So you see, Silvia is also a grandmother, and I am a great aunt by association.

Mars had a love affair with Venus, who, as you know, is associated with love and sexual desire. This was long before the seduction of Rhea Silvia and the birth of Romulus and Remus. You may be wondering where I am going with this. Let me remind you about free love in the sixties. Let me remind you of the long formal gown I wore, of the black strapless bra and the bikini panties to match, of the silk hose and the open-toed high heels, all chosen to impress my date and all eventually removed with his expertise and my implicit cooperation. I sometimes wonder what our children could have been like, Marty's and mine, but I will settle for Auntie.

Gourmet Cooking

❃

DARLENE LOOKS BEYOND THE EDGE of the campus to the gulls floating over the nearby river, then reaches for the gold-plated knocker. She is arriving early to help prepare the bastilla and the other Moroccan dishes.

She prays that his wife will not appear on the other side of the door, and her prayers are answered. He greets her with a modest grin and she scrutinizes his dark blue eyes, looking for signs of ill winds blowing from within the stucco house. She looks past the long hair and beard and catches her breath when she sees a woman with shapeless blonde hair standing almost imperceptibly behind him. "This is my wife, Joan. Joan, Darlene."

Joan moves forward and reaches out with an awkward formality. Darlene notices an almost imperceptible tic on Joan's cheek.

Immediately Joan says to her husband, "I need to talk to you privately. I can't go through with this."

There will be other guests later in the evening: the Donaldsons, both film critics; Jack Kendrick from the History Department; and others Darlene has not heard of.

Before he talks to Joan he takes Darlene to the kitchen to get her started on a search for spices and tells her how he loves to have food out, simmering all day long. He inhales deeply as though aromas have already filled the air.

Darlene studies her professor's list and surveys the cupboard full of spices, seven narrow cradled shelves on the door. She has just barely become acquainted with oregano and basil thanks to late-night pizza binges. She shakes an envelope out of the saffron bottle and carefully unfolds it. She spreads the torn envelope with her finger to reveal a rusty red powder. There is something of the smell of ketchup here, she thinks, then rejects the idea as entirely unsophisticated. The label says it is ground stigmas from a fall flowering plant, guaranteed to impart old world flavour. She tries the cumin, which has a flatter, slightly bitter aroma. The cumin bottle boasts that Cleopatra had her cooks add a pinch to the rich sauces she requested for Mark Antony, so Darlene inhales again and is disappointed. Not her idea of an aphrodisiac.

She hears bits of her professor's conversation with Joan. "A way of strengthening a marriage ... it's a new world. Work with her on the bastilla.... You'll see." Then they discuss the drinks to be served. Joan thinks brandy would be perfect for an aperitif, and he suggests a chardonnay with the couscous. Darlene has just learned to drink a little rye with her ginger ale, which had been the drink of choice for childhood illnesses.

The professor and Joan are in the kitchen now. Joan adjusts her glasses and squints as she tries to concentrate on the recipe. "I've never used filo sheets before!"

"Don't worry about that now," he says. "Start with the chicken."

"I like to know everything before I start."

"Trust me," he says. "I'll go get the wine."

Darlene shrugs her shoulders and waits for Joan to make a move. Joan is also a professor and works with laboratory rats at the university. She keeps careful data sheets, and Darlene knows she has a reputation for holding a reign of terror over her graduate assistants. Right now she looks defeated by bastilla.

"Go ahead, Darlene. You probably know a little something about this."

"No, I've never done this sort of thing." She reads the recipe. "Brown the chicken in oil. Oh, we need onions. Heart, liver, gizzard. Eew."

"You have to cut up the chicken first."

"I don't know how."

"I'll do it," says Joan. She clears out the innards, grabs the butcher knife, and begins with the thighs, cutting fiercely through to the ribs. She works quickly, hacking and stretching and pulling and sometimes slicing cleanly.

Darlene is surprised at the abandon with which Joan is attacking this chicken. She expected her to be more precise, more clinical in her dissection.

"He really is a special man," says Joan. "Very unique!"

Darlene pours oil in the pan and heats it on the gas stove. They throw pieces of chicken in and flinch at the sizzle. Joan grabs the handle and begins to shake the chicken, but most of it already sticks to the pan. Her cheeks are flushed. Darlene passes the tongs, and Joan pries each piece away from the bottom.

"I'll chop the onions and heart and all that stuff," says Darlene. "We have to cook it all in the pan once the chicken is browned."

"So, you are doing very well together," says her professor, who has just returned with the wine.

"It's all a matter of opinion," says Joan. "All right, what's next?"

"Uh, add the spices and some water, and put the chicken back in," says Darlene. She turns and smiles, studying her professor's eyes. He reminds her of John Lennon.

He puts a lid on the pan. "Just needs to simmer for a while. Let's have a sherry."

Darlene tried pot for the first time the week before. She sat with other students feeling raunchy and loose, sharing a joint and listening to *Abbey Road* on cassette while cartoon images formed in her mind.

Now the smell of Morocco wafts through the air. He puts a record on. "Miles Davis," he says. "From *Bitches Brew*." Sherry is poured from a crystal bottle as Darlene sits at the end of the plush green sofa. She takes a sip and is taken aback by the burning sensation as it spreads from her lips. She looks straight ahead, uncomfortable without a chicken to deal with.

Joan chooses an upright, firmly padded brocade chair while her husband sits next to Darlene, his legs sprawled out in front of him. "I don't like seeing the two of you together," says Joan.

"You have just spent the last hour or so together and you're getting along just fine."

"I said I don't like seeing the *two of you* together."

"Hey. I'm here for you. I haven't left."

Darlene lets the sherry ride up on her lips and sizzle there for a while. She pulls her knees up close to her chest, rests her bare feet on the sofa, and presses closer to the end of it. She studies the raised velvety swirls in the fabric, follows a path from one large button to the next, and traces the roped edges of her cushion. She finds a frayed edge on her jeans and straightens each thread so that they all run in the same direction. She realizes for the first time that her professor is wearing brown leather sandals. The straps weave in and out across the top of his foot, and his long gangly toes protrude in an unseemly manner. He and Joan are talking, but she doesn't hear what they are saying.

"I'm going for a walk," says Joan. "I need to be alone."

"She'll be all right. You'll see," he says to Darlene. "Come, we're going to make a salad together. Radish and orange salad."

"Really?"

"You'll like it. First, we'll put on *The Rite of Spring*. Stravinsky." He surrounds her easily with his arms. He strokes her hair.

Darlene thinks of singing along with Mick Jagger instead and gyrating under strobe lights to driving rhythms. Her professor pulls her close and runs his hands up and down the inside of her sweater as they listen to the whirling and booming and trilling of music, the pulsating of drums. She wonders what Joan knows about Stravinsky's ritual dance. She pulls away from him.

"The salad," she says. "I want to make the salad." She heads back to the kitchen, grabs two navel oranges, and holds them out to him. "What do we do?"

He flashes an uneasy smile and takes both oranges in one hand. "You peel them in layers."

"How?" She wonders how you peel an orange in layers. She's only ever seen them come in sections. Onions come in layers.

"I'll show you." He takes a sharp pointed knife and begins by slicing off the end, just missing the orange flesh but neatly removing the white fibre. He pulls off the rest of the peel and a bubble of juice oozes from one section.

"So now you have sections." She shrugs.

"Not so fast. First you take off the outer membrane." He holds the paring knife as she imagines a surgeon might do. With the point he separates the membranes from the flesh then gently yanks them apart. He removes the stringy core and then, with a broad grin, puts a section, with sweating juices, into his mouth.

These are not neat little layers, she thinks. But she giggles as he offers her a section. An orange has never tasted so good.

They are startled by the strains of a Strauss waltz and by Joan. "Can you believe that a hundred years ago this piece was considered licentious?"

Darlene envisions the aristocracy dancing with polished decorum. *But lords and ladies were allowed their mistresses and lovers, were they not?*

"I'll have another sherry," says Joan, and the professor pours one for himself as well.

"I think it is justifiable that you invited the Donaldsons this evening," Joan says to her husband.

"Why is that?"

"Well, since we are moving in new directions, I might as well tell you."

"Tell me what?" He is attentive.

She takes a good swig of sherry. "Stan and I are not just friends. At least we weren't last year."

Darlene studies the two of them. His pants are too short and his hair is greying and bordering on stringy at the back. His eyebrows have lowered and become rigid. Joan is like a hissing cat, in charge of her doorstep. She asks, "Didn't you know?"

"What are you saying?"

"I'm saying that we did it together."

"I don't believe you. You're just being vindictive."

"Well, yes. But I am also telling the truth."

"Then why didn't I know?" he demands. "Where?"

"On the river bank. Coming back from a walk. You guys had gone on ahead. I didn't think you could handle it if I told you. Am I right?"

"Jesus," he says and slumps into a chair.

Darlene, now even more anxious, waves a bunch of red radishes. "I'll prepare these if you tell me what to do."

"There's a grater," says Joan with a new level of confidence. "Clean them and grate them coarsely."

"And that's it?"

"Yes. Then you just add the oranges, sugar, and lemon juice, and mix it all together. It really is quite delicious."

Darlene hears voices coming from the other room, but she can't make out the words. The music has stopped. She hears her own grating of radishes and likes the rhythm of it. The chicken still simmers and occasionally spits sauce onto the burner. She smells the onions and ginger that are enhancing the chicken. She looks at the checkerboard floor and the white enamelled cupboards, pretending this is her kitchen. She imagines herself sharing wine and conversation around a candlelit table. She offers up a serving of her chicken-and-egg mixture encased within delicate layers of filo pastry and topped with almonds and sprinkles of cinnamon and sugar. She plays her choice of music, probably a piano concerto. She wears a long white cotton gown and lets her hair tumble down her back in soft curls. She is barefoot, and the guests are beguiled by her combination of innocence and sophistication. The professor and even Joan glow with admiration.

Darlene looks out the windowed back door, seeing movement there. The colony of gulls with their black wing tips and unhinging jaws are still cruising the area just outside the kitchen. She opens the door and hears them wail and squawk, drowning out her piano concerto. Drawn to the spruce and the budding poplars along the banks, the birds sail down to the river's edge, testing the frigid waters and previewing spots for nests; the young ones are courting, the mature ones re-establishing monogamous pair-bonds. Instead of her imaginary gown, Darlene fingers the familiar cotton-spun tension of her blue jeans. She leaves the kitchen and walks to the edge of the bank. This is presumably where Joan's adultery took place. Darlene walks through dead grass and brown thorny roses, then slips and slides down the muddy bank. The mud feels smooth and certain, and the air smells of spruce and mouldy winter leaves. She alternately runs and slides and stumbles, picking up speed, scraping her backbone, and scratching the skin on her arms and hands.

The river moves swiftly from spring run-off. It bubbles and foams at the edges. It carries ducks and geese heedlessly through minor swells and around unpredictable bends. She continues on down until she reaches a narrow pathway. Houses are no longer in view. She follows the path with mud oozing into her shoes. She reaches a fork; the wider path heads gently up the bank and comes to the main road that encircles the campus. She pauses. She sees the new crop of high-rises on campus as an alien might. Voices, innocent and serene, sing "Blowin' in the Wind." She quickens her step. The smell of pizza is in the air.

No Regrets

❊

CALVIN ALWAYS ASKED, "No regrets?" Now I use it as my mantra. *No regrets, no regrets, no regrets.* Like that, over and over and over.

I met him over the radio. By day he was a psychologist. He had the mustache and beard but looked more like Lenin than Freud. I didn't know what he looked like, of course, when we first hit it off. I needed to wind down after my evening shift at the hospital so I tuned in and there he was moonlighting with his mellifluous voice, kept low key for the midnight crowd. He seemed like God's gift to the intricacies of jazz, especially swing and gypsy, always describing propulsive or languid rhythms. (He claimed to have been somewhat of a gypsy in his younger days, following bands across Europe before settling on Freud.) But his analytic take on every composition, referring to dreams or unconscious associations, was all speculative. Bullshit, really. That's the reason I got involved in the first place, not realizing he was a real psychologist. I called in to protest his comment that clarinetists have an oral fixation. I am proof against that falsehood. I explained my stint in the high school band. I told him that I had never sucked my thumb, never bit my nails.

He said that I had a seductive voice. Then he put me on hold while he spun a Django Reinhardt anecdote for his listeners. We arranged our rendezvous with "My Sweet" playing on the radio. It was, for me, surreal.

This is where we first met in the flesh. Spiros has always been my favourite place. It reminds me of the Mediterranean, not that I've ever been there. Calvin gave me D. H. Lawrence's *The Virgin and The Gypsy* to read and said I should try to use my instincts and intuition more and not be so uptight. I guess he still thought himself part gypsy. He must have thought I needed a new kind of education, to be saved from certain small-town constraints, just as Lawrence's spellbinding gypsy transformed the oppressed and virginal Yvette. Though the gypsy was older and married, he was free spirited, kind of like Calvin. He saved Yvette's life from a deluge, and while enduring that flood she learned to "be braver in the body." She stopped obsessing about him as well.

In the end water was a factor. They pulled Calvin out of Lake Windermere (he was on vacation). Somehow, the driver, his wife, jumped out just in time, but Calvin's door apparently jammed. There was an on-air memorial service so I felt like I was part of the farewell. They had an archival bit with Stéphane Grappelli. They played Django's "Tears" and compared the percussive sounds of the guitars and the diminished arpeggios to Calvin's irrepressible love of gypsy jazz.

And I have my mantra.

Svea

THERE'S A PHOTO of my cousin next to her namesake, Moder Svea, a bronze statue in Berga Memorial Park in Linköping, Sweden. It bears the inscription *On Guard for the Motherland*. In the photo, our Svea is blonde and already a little buxom for a twelve-year-old. Unbeknownst to her she will soon be motherless and on guard for her younger twin sisters, Lilly and Anna. She will be on a flight with her father and sisters over the North Pole to Winnipeg, then on a CN train to Edmonton, where we will pick them up.

That was the year that Ingemar Johansson knocked out heavyweight champion Floyd Patterson, and my father and Uncle Peter celebrated their arrival by listening to the fight and getting stinking drunk. Svea looked to my mother with sheepish eyes. My mother sent us outside to have a picnic on the lawn.

We ate peanut butter and banana sandwiches, which was a first for Svea and her sisters and became their favourite for months to come. After we overheard Uncle Peter waxing on about Swedish royalty, we turned our picnics into royal affairs. In 1958 the remains of mad King Erik XIV, who apparently lost *his* mother before the age of two, were examined and found to contain high levels of arsenic; it had probably been added to his final bowl of pea soup. There was also evidence of a blow from a sword. He died in 1577, a year that was a total abstract in our girlish minds; it fell into that vague era of "the olden days." At Svea's urging we drank "arsenic water" from the garden hose to accompany our sandwiches, being royal to the core.

Death was a popular subject for the twins. They liked to lie prostrate and still on the grass for as long as possible while we used dandelion flowers and long blades of grass to tickle them back to life. They still had half notions that their mother would reappear.

It was fun to have them stay at first. Being an only child I fancied having sisters, and Svea and I each had a curly-haired twin to possess and lead around. We often competed over who would claim Lilly or Anna for the day. It depended on which twin seemed the most chirpy or malleable at the time. But eventually I yearned to have my own room back, to have my parents' undivided attention, and to resume my favoured status in our home.

And, like King Erik's father, Gustav I, Uncle Peter soon took up with a Margaret, though his Margaret was not a noble woman like Gustav's Margareta, who Gustav actually married. We called her Margareta when adults were not around, but she was really just plain old Margaret Strand, widow of Albert Strand, left to manage the Strand movie theatre and rumoured to have special showings up in the projection booth. Uncle Peter, who seemed unable or unwilling to manage a place of his own, moved into Margaret's modest two-storey Victorian, and Svea, Lilly, and Anna became well versed in movies of the late fifties and early sixties before they were of age. Lilly and Anna often reported seeing their mother in movie scenes. Uncle Peter got a job at the Creamery and worked at the Strand on weekends. Svea became chief cook and bottle washer (Margaret was not known for her housekeeping as it turned out) as well as surrogate mother to the twins. I remained the slightly naïve only child, with few responsibilities. Svea was way ahead of me in so many ways.

While they sat at the Strand (the twins armed with colouring books and crayons to keep them from watching) they saw movie queens like Elizabeth Taylor in incomprehensible films such as *Suddenly, Last Summer*, in which Elizabeth was institutionalized for mental illness after witnessing her cousin being ripped to shreds by a swarm of Spanish boys. At the urging of her aunt, Katharine Hepburn, Elizabeth faced a lobotomy. Katharine Hepburn tried to nullify the fact that her son had lured young boys for sexual favours until he tired of them and refused to give them more money. He was cannibalized as a result. It was all very weird. Then young brain surgeon, Montgomery Clift, saved Elizabeth Taylor with a serum that allowed her to bear the truth of it all. Svea told me all about it in detail. Who knew men could favour boys? Who knew boys could eat men?

By contrast I was allowed to watch Sandra Dee in *Gidget*, which was all about her teenage crush on James Darren. Sandra tried to make James jealous by throwing herself at Cliff Robertson; she dabbled with the idea of losing her virginity to Cliff as an appeal to James. Of course she didn't follow through, and James Darren gave her his class pin. I looked forward to getting a class pin myself once I went to high school.

I wanted to be sweet Sandra Dee. Svea wanted to be glamorous, sexual, on the brink of danger Elizabeth Taylor. Lilly and Anna thought maybe their mother was being held in an institution with a hole in her brain, which would explain why she had not yet reappeared. All this in spite of the fact that I, unlike Sandra Dee, had dark hair and had never kissed a boy, and Svea had blonde hair, unlike Elizabeth Taylor, and actually felt sorry for Debbie Reynolds who looked a bit like Svea's mother and whose husband, Eddie Fisher, had been stolen by Elizabeth. And this, in spite of the fact that we had explained to the twins that their mother was in heaven and would not be back on earth but would see them again much much later when they were really really old.

Svea already had the body of a woman, curvaceous and motherly—you could imagine her consoling boys and girls alike. In fact she embraced Anna and Lilly with fierce devotion. Amongst thirteen-year-olds, however, she seemed a little fat. In our minds she was bigger than a teenage girl should be. Although I couldn't read the minds of sixteen-year-old boys, they seemed to fall for the likes of Elizabeth Taylor and our Svea. Apparently so did married men.

In a funny twist, around age fourteen, Svea decided to change her name to Sandra in order to fend off comments about her unusual (to us) name. Her accent, however, could never be displaced. Years later when Britt Ekland, who only changed a vowel (Eklund to Ekland), became the token sexy Swedish blonde, famous for marrying and divorcing Peter Sellers, for becoming a Bond girl, and for later cohabitating with the mod Rod Stewart—Svea was already back to being Swedish full tilt. She was no longer the bigger girl with the big heart. We all passed through puberty and caught up to her size, developing hips and breasts like our mothers. She had already abandoned Sandra to become Svea again. It was cool to be a Swedish blonde.

Svea, of course, proved to be far too mature for the boys in high school. She already knew the complexities of caring for young children, of anticipating Uncle Peter's benders, of skirting Margaret Strand's propensity for finagling them all. By the time Britt Ekland was in the tabloids and I was off to university and other girls were going to nursing school or beauty school or agricultural college, Svea was holding the fort, waitressing at Max's Café by day, helping the twins with homework or cruising with Randy Fuller in his Ford pickup truck at night. Randy lived west of town on his parents' cattle farm, but he was often away working on the rigs for weeks at a time; it was part of his plan to finance his eventual takeover of the farm upon his parents' retirement. We all assumed that Svea would end up on that farm as well.

It's sad to say, but Svea was the victim of town gossip, and Randy was unable to ignore it all, perhaps with good reason.

Working in Max's Café exposed Svea to people in town and from miles around, and her easy sensuality did not go unnoticed. Though she had little known reason to hang out at Lens Menswear, the story goes that she had slipped in there right at the end of a day and that a last-minute customer had walked into that store, after closing time, to find Svea bent over the oak desk at the back, naked from the waist down. She had been seduced by a married man. After ordering his coffee, he would compliment her daily on her elegant posture and her sultry hip sway. She had been curious about his abilities. For Svea it would have been but a blip on the radar if it had gone undetected. Afterwards, she maintained her usual poise at work, which helped keep some suspicious minds in check, but at home Uncle Peter, in his inebriated and embarrassed state, upbraided her to the point of sending her fleeing back to our house. Randy Fuller was soon engaged to another woman. Too soon by most people's reckoning. That was the year that Elizabeth Taylor married Richard Burton after she starred in *Cleopatra* and cheated on Eddie Fisher.

  The shock for me wasn't that Svea was having sex. I already knew about her and Randy. It was that image of Svea being exposed and, more to the point, being watched. There were too many details told for just a fleeting glimpse.

  This brought Anna and Lilly full circle back to our house. The twins were used to following Svea, and by this time they were tired of the misdoings between their father and Margaret Strand. I became the weekend visitor, going from a shared room in university residence to a spot on the couch at home. My mother became their substitute mother, and Uncle Peter knew in his heart that it was for the best. The twins had just turned thirteen. You might think, given the times, that they would be a challenge to their father and to my parents, but family scandal can have a sobering effect and can even encourage conservative behaviour, at least for a time.

  My mother determined that Svea was a born nurturer, as if

she had a choice in the matter, and advised both Svea and Uncle Peter of the new nursing aide program in Edmonton, and that it would be a crime if Svea did not go. The next fall Svea and I found a basement apartment near Whyte Avenue. Sandra Dee was long gone in my head, and Julie Christie, with her wide sensual mouth, was her replacement. I wanted to be Lara to someone's Doctor Zhivago. Now we were both identifying with "the other woman," although a fraternity pin and some kind of commitment would not have been out of the question for me. That gadfly Britt Ekland was the "party girl" in *Do Not Disturb* at this point, then the kid sister, Gina, to Peter Sellers in *After the Fox*. It would be another nine years before she played the assistant to Roger Moore in *The Man with the Golden Gun*. That about measures the time it took for Svea to make her final transformation, going from bedpans during the week and party girl or devoted sister on weekends to full-time medical assistant and eventual clinic director.

I know. She surprised us all. Her qualities, that we all took for granted, of courage in the face of loss and judgement, sensitivity to the needs of others, quiet responsibility, and thicker skin than her fresh-faced aura implied set her up for managerial success. And she was determined to have a better life for herself. I, of course, had taken it all for granted.

Elizabeth Taylor had divorced and remarried Richard Burton, but I don't think Svea cared too much anymore. While Elizabeth relied on serial marriages, we rode the wave of the sexual revolution with serial dating.

Svea's new venture began with The Pill, which was first prescribed by Dr. Jensson, who she deemed less judgemental than Canadian-born doctors. Before long Dr. Jensson had a parade of Svea's friends and acquaintances, including myself, going through his office. Then Dr. Jensson, who obviously recognized Svea's strengths, hired her as his aide. This may seem inappropriate in this day and age, but it all made sense to us at the time, and it was on the up and up between the two. This was how Svea began to "associate," that is go out with, medical sales and marketing associates who came to the office to promote their wares. This was how she learned about balloon-catheter-inspired IUDs, and how she determined that women could be free of The Pill's high-dosage side effects such as weight gain and nausea and blood clotting, weight gain being her major issue. She was fitted with the Dalkon Shield (a source of sadness and irony for the rest of her life) but kept abreast of the latest pill packaging. Ads promoted the "perfect pack" and the "dial pack," and there was the addition of placebos to round out all the days of the month and maintain a regular intake by forgetful women. Options and forms of birth control marketing interested her.

The tipping point came when Uncle Peter, with his ever-increasing alcoholic flush, cut ties with Margaret Strand and her ever-increasing jaundice eyes and moved with the twins to a two-bedroom bungalow with a fenced-in backyard of his own. He was free of the Strand on weekends, but the girls were left too much on their own. Soon Anna was pregnant and came to live in our basement suite in Edmonton while Lilly stayed in school with Svea's advice and Dr. Jensson's prescriptions to protect her. Svea took on as much of the guilt as anyone. She had failed to pass on her knowledge to the twins. It dawned on her that there were countless young women, and young men too, who needed information and care. Dr. Jensson, who had promoted the idea many a time, obtained a new government grant and, along with Svea, established a birth control clinic on the edge of the university campus. It was not without controversy, but there were plenty of subscribers. Free prophylactics were a steady draw, and medical marketing firms recognized that supplying the clinic with a multitude of samples was a great way to drum up business later on. Eventually students would find jobs and pay for these familiar products.

In 1984 Elizabeth Taylor organized and hosted the first AIDS fundraiser, Britt Ekland published a fitness book called

Sensual Beauty, and Svea began a low-key campaign against the Dalkon Shield, calling into radio talk shows whenever the topic touched on birth control, pregnancy, infertility, or false and dangerous pharmaceutical advertising to women. She not only had the depth of experience from the defunct birth control clinic (grants had been phased out), she was also devastated by the device's effects on her own body. Svea, earth mother to her sisters and the sisters of others, and Aphrodite to countless men, was infertile due to the Dalkon Shield's faulty design and shady promotion. A multitude of lawsuits supported her stance in the following years.

I was never comfortable with controversy. Julie Christie (dubbed the anti-goddess) with her simmering energy and ongoing affair with Warren Beatty, haunted me from time to time, but even so I cozied into the life of a teacher, a wife, and a mother of two spirited boys. Anna, single mother of sweet Emmy, who was curly-haired like her mother, went back to school; she earned scholarships and a degree in dental hygiene, ensuring her own marketability. Lilly became a lawyer advocating for women's rights, inspired by Svea's slow but sure awakening to the roles of sex and fertility in women's lives.

And remember that farm boy, Randy Fuller, who dropped Svea over her menswear scandal? He had an awakening of sorts as well. His hurt pride had not held a candle to the pain of being married to a woman he truly disliked, the one he had hastily married after Svea's notorious fuck (as women now freely call it), bent over that desk in Len's store. Svea met up with Randy at our school reunion. Along with others he was again entranced by her goddess persona. As a woman she more fully resembled the statue of her namesake Moder Svea (Mother of Swedes). She was no longer the young girl in the photo who was destined to fly to Canada, clueless about her future. With his wife gone and his children grown, Randy met with Svea as two adults can do, knowing they each have interesting flaws and a lot of history to talk about. They took a chance on marriage, Randy for a second time. Svea was soon enthralled with the breeding of purebred cattle, with identifying the udder quality of cow, and the efficacy of the semen of champion bulls. She learned to perform artificial insemination and to market embryo transplants, but mostly she remained on guard for the well-being of us all.

Rosemary

❁

WHEN ANDREW ENCOUNTERED Rosemary it was mostly déjà vu. He could not reason why. It was the morning of the spring equinox, in the east campus parking lot. Piles of grimy snow leaked onto the pavement and students wended their way around slippery ice patches and stagnant puddles.

Andrew strode, oblivious to the grime and to the notion that the sun's illumination was equal to southern climes. He carried, in his brown leather case, a copy of *Civilization and Its Discontents*, a tattered article entitled "Thomas Aquinas Revisited," and an Egg McMuffin wrapped in moisture-proof paper.

Brown hair, soft curls. That's what he noticed.

"Today is my day for gratitude," she said, "so I have a gift for you."

"Uh, I think I need my coffee. Your name has slipped my mind."

"Rosemary," she said. "And I can't tell you how much I love your class. I'm just auditing, in case you don't know."

"Ah. That explains it. So what is this?" He dangled the gift, sprigs tied together with a yellow ribbon, in the air.

"Herbs," she said. "With meaning."

"Uh huh?"

"Parsley, sage, rosemary, and marjoram."

"Not parsley, sage, rosemary, and thyme?"

"Oh, and basil too. Ha ha, thyme. I get you. Well, thyme can give you courage, that's for sure, but that's not what I wanted to convey."

"Uh huh?"

"Marjoram is a symbol of joy and happiness. It is one thing I wish for you."

Andrew considered himself lucky, even if not joyful. Lucky because his mother Grace died when he was only four and his brother Eddie had convinced him that they had been spared the tyranny of careless mothering. As a result they had learned the value of independent thinking and logic, a perspective that was particularly suited to the dialectical methods of Plato. They both, as professors, employed dialogue successfully in their classes.

He had just one photo. The black-and-white picture revealed nothing about Grace's health. Light and shadow evoked a vulnerable woman with a generous mouth and smiling eyes. Her hair fell down in soft waves. He couldn't remember its colour. Their father gave no explanation; he was a muted witness, or so it seemed.

Grace held Andrew in her arms and out toward the camera so you could see his eyelids shut in baby bliss. Eddie stood right at Grace's extended elbow, looking straight into the camera, and their sister Margie was on the other side, leaning on their mother's leg and looking off to the side. The brothers always wondered at the wayward paths that Margie had taken back in Buffalo, before her own demise.

It was therefore inexplicable that a man who prided himself on academic thought, who was perhaps stoical about his early life, a man with tenure and a wife and three kids, after four days of resistance, lifted the limp aromatic posy from his middle desk drawer and began to google the meaning of each sprig. He remembered to search for parsley, apparently a symbol of useful knowledge, for sage, obviously a symbol of wisdom, and for rosemary, meaning remembrance. Oh, and basil: something about love spells.

The sun is three quarters up, and a jet stream curves up and over to the west, encapsulating sky and earth together, before disappearing into nothingness. Andrew studies the narrow gravel road more intensely than he would city pavement. There are ruts to negotiate that are sometimes obscured by the grassy shadows of east-side ditches. Yes, there are open fields of grain—green tinged with brown, alternating with sections of yellow canola—but bushes along the wooden and barbed-wire fences probably harbour mice and snakes. He's not sure what to expect over each rise of a hill as vehicles tend to favour the middle of the road.

There is the dead-end sign that she described. He stops on the hilltop to solidify his view. There is the red barn with green shingles and a cluster of smaller sheds to match. One shed defies convention. It is painted white with a turquoise door, window frames, and shutters. The house is fifties style, two-tone, with brown on the lower half and cream above. There is no movement: no cattle grazing, no animal of any kind wandering in this yard, yet it must be the right place.

He eases downhill to where large tractor tracks have dug up the grass and soil, and where a steel gate is secured with a padlocked heavy chain. The trees are thicker here and the farmyard is out of sight. There is a second wooden gate inside that joins a second barbed-wire fence and leads to a dirt road with grasses and clover in the middle of the tracks. He gets out of his car. What the hell is he doing here anyway?

Suddenly dogs are barking and coming down the lane. With them is Rosemary on a bike. He can hear her voice but can't make out what she is saying. He feels a rush of excitement. There is no turning back.

"Hello!" she calls, slightly out of breath.

"How are you?"

"Country style security," she explains as she opens the wooden gate and proceeds to unlock the metal one.

"What are you keeping out? Wild animals?" he jokes.

"Just unwanted traffic. It's not my arrangement. Just following through for Jill and Otto."

He nods. "The owners I presume."

"Yes. Go ahead and bring your car through."

He drives through the gates and waits for her to lock up again.

"Meet you at the house," she says as she leans into the car window, and then she pedals down the lane. The black lab bounds parallel to her, and the border collie circles ahead and back as though Rosemary is the centre of the universe. Andrew idles slowly behind. Her buttocks move rhythmically against khaki shorts. He is oblivious to everything else along the way.

She stands at the top of the wooden steps and motions with a hand.

The dogs bounce around him, scrutinizing him willynilly.

"Thelma, Louise, stop that," she orders and the dogs settle down.

"Very funny," he says. "Thelma and Louise?"

"Oh, you have to know Jill and Otto," she says, laughing. "It's their sense of humour."

"Am I safe here?" he jokes.

"Safe as anywhere. Come on in. I'm just making us lunch. We can take it on our hike."

She resumes preparations at the kitchen counter, assembling and wrapping up egg salad sandwiches, oatmeal cookies, green apples, and bottled ice tea. "Hope you like all this."

"Sure, fine. Anything's fine," he says as his eyes follow the V-neck of her T-shirt downward to hidden cleavage.

She moves quickly from counter to sink and back again and looks over at him periodically to confirm their conversation. They talk about the fact that Jill and Otto are not really farmers; they are artists who maintain the farmyard and lease the fields out to neighbours.

The city, more specifically the university, recedes in a flash, as does Lois, his wife. This kitchen, with its oak table and pink cupboards and smooth black counters, possesses him. There is room for a large family and extras at harvest time, but now it is just the two of them. He needs to make a move, but something holds him back.

Birds sing a cantata through the window, punctuated by the sound of flies jotting on the screen. Time ticks away with the clock on the stove and floats out the door, swirls around the sheds, and sails over the open fields and down to the creek that apparently runs at the property's bottom edge. Life as he knows it—his immersion in books and constant family dilemmas, the strain of appeasing Lois, all float away.

"Are you ready?" she asks.

"I am!"

"I've got a couple of backpacks. Here, you take the lunch in this one. I need mine for flowers." She drops a pair of blunt-end scissors into the bottom of her pack.

"That's all you're taking?" he says.

"I'll have plenty to bring back."

They head down a mowed path toward the tree line where the creek is hidden from view. They reach an open meadow. Butterflies, radiated by sunlight, flit from a stack of logs to the grass and back again. They walk past dry anthills and listen to grasshoppers. Soon they hear water trickling further down. They look down a steep bank to the muddy creek and negotiate their way through low-lying scrub and young poplars. Wild raspberries and strawberries and mushrooms abound.

"Have a raspberry." It sits like a gemstone in her hand.

He drops another in his mouth. "Barely a taste. A teaser!"

"Oh here, forget-me-nots!" She pulls out her scissors and snips a stem. The flower is composed of sky blue petals and a yellow eye. "There's a legend about them," she says.

"And what is that?"

"Well, a woman and her lover were walking along a river

when she spied a beautiful blue flower. She asked if he would get it for her, and of course he wanted to please her. However, he lost his footing and fell in, crying out with his dying words—'forget me not, forget me not.'"

"Aren't you the romantic."

They move closer to the water, on boggy clay, amongst horsetails and a crop of white daisies. They have to watch their step. A beaver dam explains the slow-moving water. She pulls out her scissors again. "I want the best daisies I can get. Here let me hand them to you."

They move further down to where larger rocks create a gentle rippling in the water and flat rocks invite them to walk across to the other side. "Shall we try it?"

He hears movement in the bushes. Some small creature. It causes him to pause.

"Come on. Don't be shy." She heads across the water.

He lurches after her and slips, losing balance, his arms flying with daisies in one hand, his legs slashing the water, his bottom suddenly resting on the rocky bed.

"Are you all right?"

"Jesus," he replies.

She sounds like a pan flute when she laughs.

He pulls himself out of the water, holding the sopping daisies up to dry air. "Here, come and get your flowers." He is looking full of mischief now. Egging her on.

She reaches for the bouquet while he takes a step away. Her foot slips, just as his had, and she takes the plunge. They giggle like teenagers and splash each other with uncoordinated swipes. Daisies float in all directions.

"Hey, what about our lunch?"

"Oh yeah," he replies. "Better save it." And he gives her one last dose of water in her face. "Here, take my hand. I'll help you out."

"No way!" She scrambles out herself. Her clothes cling nicely.

They move to higher ground.

"So much for daisies." He smiles and takes off his shirt. His khaki pants cling heavily to his legs. "Well, enough of this." He takes off his pants; his boxers are still dry in places. "Feel free to do the same."

"No, that's all right. The sun will dry me."

He hangs his pants over a branch and clenches his arms in a body builder's pose.

"Oh you." She zips open the backpack and pulls out the bag of food. "It seems okay."

They sit side by side and look back across the creek to the steep banks. It is like someone with a giant knife has sliced straight down, revealing layers of clay and rock and coal and eroded soil.

"It must have been a deep river eons ago," he says.

A bird interrupts, horning in on all the others with two clear long whistles followed by three quarter notes. It repeats itself.

"You hear that?"

"What?"

"That whistling?" He whistles out the tune.

"White-throated sparrow," she says. "Dear old Canada Canada Canada, he's saying."

"You're sure about that?"

"Positive."

He smiles to himself and listens some more. "Could be saying dear old America America America you know."

"Absolutely not. Too many syllables."

"Hmph. And I suppose you want to look for daisies again."

"I am counting on them."

"Or counting them. Isn't that what you do? Count daisy petals? He loves me, he loves me not."

"Ha. Actually those aren't really petals. Each white so-called petal is an individual flower, and the yellow center is made up of tiny florets that contain both stamens and pistils. When you pick a daisy you pick a bouquet."

"Just the same. I'll bet you've done that."

"Well, sure, when I was young. Until I learned that, like many things, it can be fixed."

"How so?"

"There is usually an uneven number of white petals."

"I thought you said they weren't petals."

"Just for the sake of communication."

"Fine."

"As I was saying, there is an uneven number, so if you start with 'he loves me' you end up with 'he loves me.' Kind of takes the fun out of it, don't you think?"

"Well I wouldn't be counting on that sort of thing anyway. How about you? Any big romance in your life? Seems a woman like you…"

"Want to know more about daisies?"

"Do I have a choice?"

"The name comes from 'day's eye,' because a particular English variety closed at nightfall and opened again at sunrise. It was also called 'thunder flower' because it was always around during spring showers and was thought to be protective. People hung daisies indoors for protection from lightning."

"Thunder-flower. I like that. Now I know why you're really collecting them."

"Definitely. Protection from any storm. You might want to take some home for yourself."

"Oh ho. You think my home life is stormy? You think I'll be struck by lightning?"

"Perhaps."

Time shifts in unknown currents. Memory, caught in a sluggish pool, is suddenly released. Visions of Grace with her tender eyes and ephemeral embrace flash uninvited. Grace, his mother, appears like lightning. This is simply trumped up memory, he thinks. Childish wishful thinking. He is not taken in by it. Truth trickles like water down the creek, sometimes resting stagnant in a pool, sometimes bubbling into eddies and ripples of light, always on the move.

She smiles and looks somewhere far away. "A little bit like heaven here, don't you think?"

"Yeah," he whispers and turns his head away. A tear drop is forming unannounced. He quickly wipes it away.

"Something on your mind?" she asks. "Anything I can do?"

"Nah."

She offers another forget-me-not that she has plucked from the grasses just within her reach. "There's another story. You might like it better."

"And what is that?"

"It's an old German folk tale. A young man spots a little blue flower in the mountains. He veers from his path to get it, and he finds himself at the entrance of a cave full of treasures. As he stuffs his pockets full of gold and jewels, a beautiful woman appears. Why she has to be beautiful is beyond me. However, she warns him by saying, 'Forget not the best.' He, of course, leaves the little blue flower, the forget-me-not, behind, not realizing it is the best treasure of all. As he leaves the cave, rocks from the mountain come crashing down, killing him and closing up the cave forever."

"Well that's very uplifting."

"You talked about Plato's cave in your class. Consider it another cave story."

"Hah."

"I really would like to get more of those daisies since they are in such good form right now."

They gather up the remains of lunch. Andrew pulls his pants back on even though they are still damp, and they head back to the creek, moving in unison, offering a hand when it is needed, reaching and clipping and gathering *day's eyes* in abundance.

They head to the white shed, the one with the turquoise trim, with daisies peering out of their open backpacks and cradled in their arms. It is cool and shadowy inside. The windows are shuttered but some light manages to creep in. Along the walls flowers are hanging upside down from protruding nails, bundled together with twine.

"Here, bring those over here." She sets her daisies down on an old chrome table. "I need to prepare them for drying right away. Have to preserve the freshness."

"Kind of contradictory, don't you think?"

"What's that?"

"Drying to preserve freshness?"

"Well, nothing lasts forever. I'm just preserving something at its peak."

"Is it really the same though?"

"Of course not. But it has its own beauty. When you think about it, books preserve someone's ideas. Even if they become outdated they can still illuminate a certain truth. It's all fleeting, but some moments in life just need to be preserved."

"Getting philosophical?"

"Here, you. I'll put you to work." She demonstrates the trimming of stems and the binding together of small bouquets with twine for hanging from the ceiling. "See? You just clean off the lower part." She holds a daisy up for him to see, her eyes searching his.

He must make a move, but he feels short of breath, a little tipsy. He is nervous but he can't figure out why. "I'm going to have to run," he says.

"Of course," she replies. "I'll open up the gates."

He plays Arrowsmith's "Dream On" as he makes his way back to the city. Steven Tyler is singing his own lyrics and Andrew tries to sing along.

At night he dreams that he is at a restaurant with Eddie. The restaurant has private booths laid out in labyrinthine fashion. They choose a booth that is isolated from both customers and staff. There are copies of *The Republic of Plato* at each table. The brothers seem to be waiting for someone. They have not ordered any food. A woman finally arrives and focuses her attention on Andrew, although she remains standing closer to Eddie. As they talk the woman becomes more and more like Rosemary. She is Rosemary. Suddenly Andrew realizes that she has arranged to meet Eddie, not him. Then Eddie asks, "Are you my mother?" Andrew realizes, with clarity, what he should have known all along. This mother abandoned Eddie and now has agreed to meet him again. "I'm so sorry," says Andrew. "I didn't realize that you have been without a mother all this time."

He wakes up with the strangest feeling. The picture book, *Are You My Mother?* is on his bedside table. He read it to his children the night before. The little bird, who had fallen out of his nest and become separated from his mother, went around asking the strangest characters, both animate and inanimate, "Are you my mother?"

It becomes an ear worm, like a pop song being recycled on the radio. He makes a game of it in an effort to control his thinking. Like the little lost bird, he chooses the strangest objects and says under his breath, "Are you my mother?" He asks the Manitoba maple at the end of his driveway, the neighbour's pregnant Irish Setter who had been taken out for a short morning walk, the girl pumping gas at Turbo on the boulevard, the poplar being pruned in front of St. Anthony's, the traffic light at the intersection, and the gas light on the main drag with its never-ending flare.

He listens to certain predictable melodies of Mozart and Haydn to drown out details of the dream, but it persists and haunts him for several days.

Was it was all a mistake, dallying with a student, even if she was mature and had simply audited his time? He had easily had affairs in the past, but this time it remained platonic. For days in a row, tears appear at the oddest moments, making his behaviour unpredictable. He finally decides to revisit Rousseau and Kant with his summer students, perusing the notion of self-contradiction. Rosemary does not attend the class. At the end of the day, as he heads to the parking lot, he stops to observe skittery sparrows as they fly out from green hedges, down to patches of water and back up again. And a white-throated sparrow, which he now can identify, whistles *Rosemary Rosemary Rosemary*. He is certain of that.

Snipe Hunting

❊

THE MOON HOVERS over Jarvis Hills and the scent of sun-dried hay mingles with evaporating manure. In the farm yard Toby bounds in circles around Ellie while the black lab and the bloodhound bark at her like inquisitors before jumping at her chest and slobbering on her shoes.

"Ooh! Get down!" she says, warding off the dogs with one hand and shielding her hair with the other. Earlier in the afternoon she put rollers in her hair according to illustrations in *Mademoiselle,* teased and combed it out to look like Sandra Dee, and then kept her head from resting in the car all the way from Calgary.

"Stop that. Down boys. Toby, get over here," says Uncle Alec. Toby, the favourite, obliges his master and wags his happy tail. The other two dogs sit by the wooden steps to guard the house. "They won't hurt you. They just get excited. Pretty young lady like you."

Maybe it's true. Perhaps she does cause excitement. Her parents are spared the rambunctious pawing as they follow her out of the white sedan and wave. Aunt Helen, a dish towel in her hand, smiles from the doorway like a deaf angel welcoming them to heaven.

Ellie's cousins, Todd and Gary, come up from the barn and shake hands with her father, kiss her mother on the cheek, and nod "hi" to Ellie. The boys seem shy at first, but Gary smiles easily, as if he is about to tell a tall tale, and his voice crackles when he turns to Uncle Alec and says, "By the way, we found more gunny sacks." He sounds like Troy Donahue in *A Summer Place*, talking about some hideaway to share with Sandra Dee.

"Good, we can use them all." Uncle Alec winks at Ellie's father; the two men are cousins, but they bonded like brothers while growing up on adjacent farms.

"We need more flashlights," says Todd. "Is Mr. Stadel bringing his over?"

"Better call and make sure," says Uncle Alec.

Aunt Helen intercepts, her hearing restored. "They said they were bringing extras and so are the Johnsons, so don't worry. Come, supper's ready."

It is already eight o'clock. They sit at the oak table and pass around fresh buns, roast chicken, coleslaw, mashed potatoes, peas and carrots cooked in cream, and last year's corn relish. "So you've never been snipe hunting, Ellie?" Uncle Alec waves a leg of chicken between mouthfuls to accentuate his enthusiasm. "It's a perfect night for it, full moon and all. Makes it easy to spot them when they run into the open. Your dad and I first went hunting for snipe on a night like this, over on Peter Hansen's farmstead." He prods Ellie's father. "Remember that?"

"Sure do," her father replies. "Old Peter came up from South Dakota. Said snipe hunting was the unofficial sport down there. Decided to pass the tradition on to us since he never had kids of his own."

Gary and Todd smile at each other and roll their eyes.

"Hey Ellie, I've got the wishbone," says Aunt Helen. She holds it out for Ellie to grasp. "Come on now, make a wish."

"I'll bet she bags a snipe first time out," says Gary as he winks at Ellie.

"Yep. I can see luck, like a halo, circling that pretty head," Uncle Alec adds.

"Let her make her wish," says Aunt Helen.

Ellie stares out the kitchen window, over the red barn and the rusty windmill, to see a moon that is ready to burst. She foresees massive fireworks, iridescent pastures, and blackened poplars. Male snipe perform aerial dives, with their tail feathers spread in a rainbow of colours, and carry ladybugs in their long pointed bills to the females waiting in the marsh below. She looks back at Gary and Todd and can't decide. "I don't know what to wish for," she says, even though she knows this is only half true.

"How about that bike you've been wanting?" says her mother. Ellie shakes her head. Her face flushes red.

"It has to be a secret," says Todd in her defence. Todd has dark hair and a glint in his eyes that says he could suddenly turn and sing "There's No Such Thing," the way James Darren did in *Gidget*.

"Yes!" she replies then quickly makes her wish. She grasps the free end of the delicate looking, v-shaped bone and snaps her piece away from Aunt Helen. She holds it up, the largest piece, and smiles at Todd.

"I knew it. She's our lucky charm tonight," says Uncle Alec.

"I'm sticking with Ellie," says Gary.

"Come on Helen," says Ellie's mother, "let's get this cleaned up. Ellie and I will help with the dishes while the men finish up outside."

The two women commune, their voices rising above the clatter of plates and cutlery. They speculate about Helen's sister, Freda, who is getting a divorce. Ellie inhales the air of disapproval without hearing much of what they say. She is intent on tracking Gary and Todd as they pass back and forth by the kitchen window before disappearing into the dusky night, down around the barn. They might leave her behind with women who have no intention of joining the hunt.

"Come on Ellie, get that tea towel wet will you?" says her mother.

Pickup trucks and a blue sedan arrive in the yard. Aunt Helen's sister Freda, Mrs. Johnson, and Mrs. Stadel walk into the house unannounced while the two little Stadel girls run right back out to find kittens in the barn. Men and boys have already bypassed the house in favour of barnyard shadows. Ellie hovers around the window and the door. "Maybe I should go."

"Don't you worry," says Aunt Helen. "They'll be a while yet. Oh, Karen, what lovely earrings," she says to Mrs. Stadel. "Now where did you find them?"

"But they might forget me."

"Of course not, Ellie dear. Pardon me, Karen. In Red Deer? At Mitchells?"

"Who cares about stupid earrings," mutters Ellie.

"What's that, Ellie?"

"Nothing."

"Well how're the ladies?" Uncle Alec strides in and takes off his cap. He puts it on Mrs. Stadel's head, provoking giggles from the others.

"Are we going soon, Uncle Alec?"

"Soon as those boys have everything ready. You'd better put a jacket on. Gets cool out there this time of year and you still might get eaten by mosquitoes. Besides, if you don't cover up the coyotes will get romantic and start serenading you. Might want to steal you for their own. I already heard some howling out there."

"You are funny," says Aunt Helen. "Did you notice Karen's earrings under that cap, smarty Alec?"

"Yes, it's Helen's birthday coming up," adds Freda. "Hint hint."

"Let me see." He stands close to Mrs. Stadel and fingers her ears, then snatches his hat back. Her ears turn red.

"They're just regular gold earrings," mutters Ellie.

"Ah hah. So there!" says Uncle Alec. "Just your ordinary, everyday gold earrings." He tugs Ellie's ear. "I think, ladies, I'd better get back to the hunt. Come on, El."

"Send my girls in, will you Alec?" asks Mrs. Stadel.

"Will do."

The two little girls are already heading back. They stop to

gaze at Ellie, who pretends to concentrate on preparations for the hunt.

"Okay girls, on your way," says Mr. Stadel. The girls wave at Ellie as they run up to the house.

Uncle Alec begins to get things organized. "Now we need flushers and we need baggers. Gary, take the gunny sacks and the lantern. Todd, you give out the flashlights."

"Where are you going to be?" asks Todd.

"I'll be here at headquarters. Anybody needs me I'll be right here."

"But I thought you were coming." Todd frowns at his father.

"Someone has to hold the fort." Uncle Alec stands firm. He pats his shirt, looking for a match, and reveals the top of a mickey peeping out from his inside jacket pocket. He jostles Ellie's father with his elbow. "Besides we've had our turn many a time."

Todd looks away, but Gary grins and puts a gunnysack over Ricky Johnson's head. They laugh and scuffle and look to see if Ellie is watching. The Stadel boys nudge each other.

Uncle Alec continues. "Okay, we've got lots of first timers here tonight so I'm gonna give you some instructions before you head out. Gary will establish a central location for the baggers in a clearing we've got down there in the trees. He'll have the big lantern, so use that as your guide. You flushers stay in the trees, circling the lantern. You creep in to about a hundred yards from the centre, turn your lights off, and wait a while to let the critters settle down. Then Gary will give the signal by flicking his lantern on and off and you start hollering and clapping as you move toward the baggers. This'll send the snipe right toward the sacks. Just make sure you stop all the commotion before you reach the clearing so they slow down a bit. All right? So Gary will give out sacks to whoever wants to be a bagger. You've got to be on your toes to catch a snipe and keep it in your sack because they can be fast and sneaky."

Gary smiles at Ellie and offers her a sack, but she shrinks back. She imagines a bird flapping and squawking inside, poking its straw-like bill at her through the loosely woven burlap, trying anything to escape, its colourful tail feathers flying helter skelter, waiting for their opportunity to fly out.

Uncle Alec puts his hand on her shoulder. "Ellie, you best go with Todd. I think maybe you should be a flusher."

She smells whisky on Uncle Alec's breath and looks to her father for some reaction, but he has no particular expression on his face. He and Mr. Stadel stand aloof, ready to escort the neophyte flushers to their hiding spots.

"Come on Ellie. You don't need to take a flashlight. You'll be with me," says Todd.

"Now one more thing," says Uncle Alec. "Listen carefully for the flutter of wings. You know how they sound?"

Everyone either shakes their head or looks at the ground.

Gary cups his right hand to his mouth and makes a breathy call. "Woobidah, woobidah, woobidah. Woobidah, woobidah, woobidah." At the same time he bends his left arm and affects a flapping wing.

Laughter rises from the hunters as they stand outside the farmhouse window. It floats up through the Manitoba maples where the bats are swooping and flitting, over the bejewelled umbrella of the crabapple tree, and down to the pasture where the sheep begin to huddle nervously but the cattle seemed unaffected, conveniently deaf like Aunt Helen. Even Ellie's father and Todd join in the antics. Some of the boys mimic Gary: "Woobidah, woobidah, wooh."

Ellie looks high above Jarvis Hills and laughs right at the moon. Sure enough, the coyotes answer back. "Yipidah, yipidah, yip yip yip, yipidah."

She shivers. "I forgot my jacket. I'll be right back."

"Don't worry, I'll wait for you," says Todd. "Come back here, Toby. Sit. You're going with us."

Karen Stadel comes out to say goodbye, and Uncle Alec

offers her a Craven A. The two stand close together as he cups the match and she drags fire into the tip of the cigarette. "Take care, you two," she says then exhales. Ellie and Todd are headed for the pasture. "We're fine," Todd mutters, though he doesn't sound like it.

The group ahead has already reached the woods. Genial voices, punctuated by laughter, trail back to the two stragglers who are still in open pasture. As the hunters disperse amongst the trees, their voices sound conspiratorial. Twigs snap, rotting logs echo, dogwood and saskatoon bushes rustle, and prickly wild rose hips inspire minor complaints.

Toby continually runs ahead of Todd and Ellie then circles back. The two walk in suspended silence; occasionally their shoulders rub and their hands touch. They keep moving apart, only to find themselves drawn back to a narrow path in a wide-open pasture.

The air is snappy, the moon overripe, the coyotes tantalizing, and the earth unsteady like a California tremor. The two collide as Toby zips around their feet.

"Toby, cut that out. Sorry. You all right?" says Todd.

Ellie giggles. "It's okay. I don't mind. Hey Toby?" She tries to pat him on the head, but the dog is already off circling in front of them, certain to make his way back.

They enter the woods with their flashlight turned on. "We'll stay on this side since you don't have boots on," Todd says, his voice lowered. "It gets pretty wet over there." They hear Toby scurrying through the bushes, his route no longer predictable. "Look for the lantern. Should be over that way."

"I see it." She touches his arm and motions with her head. "Over there."

"Good. We'll hide in here." He grabs her hand and guides her into long grasses, near the sweeping branches of an old cottonwood tree and behind a screen of willows. He turns off the flashlight; they are nestled and alone.

Ellie, suddenly delirious, stares up through treetops to see fragments of moon framing the antics of a great snipe. He flips and dives like an acrobat, spreading his rainbow tail feathers to make a whooshing sound: *woobidah, woobidah, woobidah, wooh*. A female stays grounded below in a small clearing, bedazzled but muted by all the excitement. Then coyotes harmonize—*yip yip yip, yeowl*—and Ellie shivers.

"Are you okay?" Todd puts his arm around her.

"What colour are their tails?"

"Snipe? Oh, kind of a chestnut colour with black-and-white bands at the tips."

"Oh! And are they big birds?"

"No. Only about the size of a robin, with a short tail."

"Oh."

He pulls her close so her head rests on his chest. "Chilly, eh?"

Ellie has kissed two boys before. She was paired up with Dennis Olson, against her wishes, for Joanie Carmichael's birthday party; it was the first mixed party, which she couldn't bear to miss. When the lights went out in Joanie's rumpus room, Dennis pushed his lips and teeth onto Ellie's. She gagged and quickly found a light switch, bringing on complaints from all the others. She preferred Jeff Willoughby, who disappeared whenever the lights went off. She kissed him once though, at the skating rink, while they were playing keep-away. Caught him just as he was about to break through the guards to her side; grabbed his jacket and held on tight as he spun her in circles on the ice and teased that he would kiss her if she didn't let go. She hung on tight.

Now Todd lifts her chin and kisses her the way James Darren kissed Sandra Dee. A real kiss. Toby barks. Hunters' feet stomp the earth, crunch dead twigs, and scuttle around bushes while hands clap and voices holler, "Whooee, yipidah, yeow." Small lights flash through the trees.

"We'd better go," says Todd. "Come on." He pulls her up from the grass and runs with her towards the lantern and the baggers.

Thorns scratch her hands and saplings whip her face. She is breathless. "Hang on, slow down," she cries and he complies. "What will they do with them if they catch any? I mean, they're so small."

"I wouldn't worry too much." Todd smiles. "Come on, we'd better hurry."

The hunters rally, telling stories of crossed paths, accidents, and failed opportunities, even the occasional sighting of snipe—but no one has booty in the bag. There is laughter and complaining and even talk of flimflam. Gary revels in it all but pauses when he sees Todd and Ellie holding hands, then hollers even louder. "Come on everyone. Let's head back." Ellie's hand goes limp as they all parade back to the house, with Gary in the lead, and Todd finally lets it go.

"Hey, hey. How many did you bag?" asks Uncle Alec as he stands outside the farmhouse door, like a bouncer at the local bar. "Ah well, come on in. Hot chocolate for everyone!"

Karen Stadel goes forward to greet her boys. "How was it? Did you catch any?" she asks as she pats them on the back. Then she turns to Ellie and says, with whisky on her breath, "So, was it all you expected?"

Her two little girls come out, the youngest looking dazed, still half asleep. "I saw Ellie and Todd holding hands. I bet she's his girlfriend," says the older sister.

"Don't be silly dear," says Aunt Helen who is now in the doorway. "They're cousins after all."

"Second cousins once removed," mutters Ellie.

Toby barks and pirouettes. The black lab and the bloodhound barely open their eyes, no longer on guard at the foot of the steps.

"Go lay down, Toby. That's it for tonight," says Todd, and they all gather inside to have hot drinks.

Back in Calgary, Ellie brags to her friends, as they sit crosslegged on her bed, that she has gone hunting and she will surely hunt again.

The girls huddle over a copy of *Photoplay* in which Sandra Dee reveals that she doesn't part her hair; she lets the wind comb it to give a tousled look. Ellie intends to let her own hair fly from here on out.

GENEVA STORIES

Rockin' Around the Royal Bank of Canada

❊

FOUR BABY ROBINS STRETCH their bare necks and open their mouths toward heaven. Their nest rests on an upper window ledge of the Royal Bank of Canada, right on the corner of Neville and Main. Below, Geneva Roberts and Darla Collier arrive for Mary Stewart's thirteenth birthday party dressed in matching navy skirts and Banlon sweater sets. Mary's younger sister Janie lets them in the side door, on Neville. Diane Wedder barges right past them, up the stairs to the Stewarts' apartment above the bank.

Diane, almost two years older than the others—she failed grade seven—moved to Bradshaw with her mother and younger brother the previous summer. They rented a two-bedroom bungalow on Harley Street opposite a weed-infested vacant lot, an auto body shop, and St. Cecilia's Catholic Church, a street that Geneva Roberts rarely goes down even though she is free to roam like every kid in town.

Something about Diane is different; her mother and brother have matching red hair and freckles and compact skinny frames, while Diane is dark-haired and full-bodied. Darla says that Diane's real last name is Pickle—she overheard her mother talking—and that Mr. Wedder is locked up somewhere. Geneva has the murky feeling that something about Diane is on the shady side, *unacceptable*, like nail polish. Diane's nails, in fact, are painted cherry red for the party and her eyes are rimmed with black eyeliner.

The Stewarts' dining table is laid out in white linen with Royal Doulton plates, polished silver, and Czechoslovakian glasses filled with lemonade. Mrs. Stewart, the bank manager's wife, is giving a grown-up dinner party to mark her daughter's first day as a teenager. The attempt at sophistication subdues the party until Diane knocks over a glass and they all dash over with linen napkins to soak up the spill. Diane, in her black pedal pushers and blouse with the stand-up collar, stands aside and sings "I'm All Shook Up." The right corner of her top lip quivers and her hips gyrate. Carol Simmons cracks that Diane must have tripped in her blue suede shoes—Geneva and Darla actually check Diane's feet—then everyone erupts into giggles that resurface for no particular reason for the rest of dinner, until the angel food birthday cake is gone.

"I'm stuffed!" they all say as they drape themselves over the living room sofa and chairs or sprawl on the carpet, waiting for Mary to open her presents. Diane thrusts her gift into Mary's hands and sings, "Let me be your teddy bear."

"Ooh, I love it," says Mary as she smooshes the pink bear against her cheek.

Darla's day-of-the-week panties are a hit—the new necessity. Geneva's gift is next: a porcelain figurine, an elegant month-of-May girl with a garland of flowers crowning her golden hair. It is not what she intended to give.

Geneva and Mary were at Jamesons Drugstore the previous week where Mary obsessed over a triple pack of nail polish—pastel mauve, pastel pink, and snow-fire red—and reminded Geneva of her upcoming birthday.

When Mrs. Roberts gave Geneva the money to buy a present, Geneva knew very well that nail polish would not be on her mother's list of acceptable gifts, which is why she bought the pack and hid it in her dresser drawer, avoided her mother's eyes when asked if she had bought anything, then returned it to the drugstore, choosing instead Miss May from the china section of her father's store, Roberts Hardware. She planned to tell Mary how sorry she was, that she tried to get the polish, even bought it, but her mother *made* her return it to the store.

"She'll fit perfectly on your keepsake shelf, dear, to mark your thirteenth birthday," says Mrs. Stewart. The girls, being polite, murmur in agreement. "When you're finished with presents you can all go to the Roxy. The show starts in half an hour."

"Hurry up, Mary! Open the rest so we can go," says Diane Wedder in her gravelly voice, as though she's in charge.

The girls scuttle down the stairs and out the door. Two robins swoop and natter at them with little effect. Diane takes the lead, keeping Mary in tow, as the others skip and jostle their way up Main. Geneva and Darla purposely bring up the rear, countering Diane's rowdy influence with a studied gait. "She's so pushy," they both agree.

"Pop for everyone, popcorn too," they are told in the Roxy, and they all push forward, dismissing previous complaints about stomachs ready to burst.

Bugs Bunny wisecracks on the screen while the girls whisper and giggle, trade seats, and spill popcorn. Suddenly they are drawn to the main attraction like witnesses to divine light. It isn't the story of a band looking for a big break that pulls them in. Sandra Dee and Troy Donahue aren't there sneaking a lustful kiss that could lead to something more. It's the powerful beat, the electric charge, the crazy jitterbugging that makes them sit up, light up, and jump up. It's Bill Haley & His Comets: "Rock Around The Clock."

Diane Wedder claps her hands, bounces up and down, and dances in and out of her seat. Carol Simmons on one side of her, and Patty Schultz on the other, bounce and sway along with Diane. The other girls, including Geneva and Darla, tap their heels and rock their shoulders but stay firmly in their seats. Diane sings along as though she already knows the words.

She is still singing and shouting as they leave the Roxy. "Let's par...tee. Yeah! Rock, rock, rock." She jitterbugs down Main Street like a pied piper; even Geneva and Darla join in. She slows to flip Patty over her back as they near the bank. The two robins, Mom and Pop, are also causing a ruckus on Neville and Main, but the party girls barely hear it above their own squealing and shouting. Then Diane suddenly stops and veers away. "I gotta run home. Mary, get your record player."

The girls threaten to take their rowdiness up to the apartment as they jostle into the entrance off Neville. Mr. Stewart rushes down to meet them with a ring of keys. "Remember Mary, customer side only." With that he unlocks the double doors to the bank and, before they can say *be bop a lula*, he leads them past the tellers' cages, with the tall wooden stools and plate glass windows; past his own office with his cushioned chair, oak desk, and Olivetti typewriter; through the counter gate; and onto the polished battleship linoleum where customers usually stand in line. Mary's sister Janie brings the record player and Diane arrives with a handful of forty-fives. Bill Haley blasts out all over again.

Acrobatics rule as the bigger girls swing Geneva and Darla and Patty and Janie, who stand on chairs to get a leg up, flipping over heads and backs. Ordinary jiving takes on new twirls and dives as hands reach for shoulders and feet leap off the floor. Skirts flare up and Saturday panties flash in the overhead lights of the Royal Bank of Canada.

Diane announces, before she puts on "Great Balls of Fire," that Jerry Lee Lewis married his *first* cousin, who was thirteen, the *same* age as Mary Stewart. "Eew," the girls reply. Geneva's stomach does a small turn, confirmation of the fact that they are wading into unseemly territory. Little Richard sings "Tutti Frutti" and Elvis sings "All Shook Up" with Diane Wedder as his mimic. When the Platters calm things down with "Only You," Diane takes a turn into melancholy. As quickly as the bank had become a rock 'n' roll palladium, Diane transforms it into a funeral parlour. She turns off the record player and sings "Old Shep." Tears run down her cheeks and her voice turns nasal as the song progresses, as though someone close to her has died.

Geneva looks sideways at Darla, who, along with the other girls, has cast herself as comforter to the bereaved—to Shep's owner who, with trembling hands, shot Shep in the head, and to Diane, who seems to take it personally.

There is genuine sorrow in the air, greedily inhaled (it seems to Geneva) by Diane Wedder. Exuberance around Mary Stewart's thirteenth birthday party is fully depleted; communal piety soars with the promise that Old Shep is now in heaven. Diane cries, "I have to go," as she rattles the main door. "Let me outta here. Someone unlock the door!" Mr. Stewart is called to set them free.

Out on the sidewalk lies a tiny specimen, beak permanently closed, eye staring sideways, veins bulging through translucent skin and partially squished to the cement. The girls draw back. "Eew," is all they can say while two robins harangue from above and three mouths still reach out of their nest toward heaven.

Roberts Hardware is abuzz with customers on Monday morning when farmers, desperate to finish planting grain before forecasted rain, rush in to buy replacement parts for ailing cultivators and seeders, and Bradshaw's housewives, in the throes of spring cleaning, discover their brooms and wash pails are ratted or leaking and coincidentally they need to buy Royal Albert cups and saucers for the upcoming bridal shower. Geneva hangs at the back of the store until Mrs. Roberts takes bills from the till, makes a list of currency, and places it in a cash sack. "I need you to run to the bank and get some change."

Diane Wedder's brother is loitering on the bank steps, his red hair ruffled, his mouth pressed into a sardonic twist. His eyes, however, widen with puppy optimism as Geneva approaches, offers up her smile, and says, "Hello." He's a fifth grader so she understands his admiration; she passes him with an air of great intention to do business with the bank.

As she stands in line, Geneva spots Mrs. Wedder through the manager's window, sitting across the desk from Mr. Stewart, her bony frame at odds with the hard oak chair. Mr. Stewart, bolstered by his royal blue cushion, leans back and, with a sober shrug, raises his empty hands, palms up. Mrs. Wedder stands up, her face as red as her hair, and rushes toward the counter. A teller circles around to unlock the gate and set her free.

Mrs. Wedder brushes past Geneva and barks at her son. "I told you to wait outside," she says, and the boy grins at Geneva, pretending nothing is amiss. "He can go to hell," she spits and the boy ducks his head as if he is the target. (Geneva's mother would say *he can go to Halifax* instead.)

A teller calls, "I can help you now, Geneva," so Geneva turns away to trade the hardware cash.

On the following Sunday, Geneva, Darla, and Mary Stewart sit in the very back pew, separate from their parents, in St. Stephen's Anglican Church. A month before they paraded in white dresses and veils, looking like angels or juvenile brides, and tasted their first sip of holy red wine. Today they squelch their giggles for their second communion, kneel with their hands cupped towards heaven, and wait for a sacred wafer to be deposited by Reverend Hill. Geneva turns from the altar and sees Mrs. Wedder with her son, mere witnesses to Holy Communion. The congregation sings "Blessed Assurance," but when she bursts out of the church, Geneva whispers Bill Haley's tune with its promise to be in "seventh heaven."

Outside Reverend Hill has Mrs. Wedder's hand sandwiched between both of his—she rushed out as quickly as the girls—only letting go when others follow along to praise the day. As she breaks away, her son looks backward, catching Geneva's eye.

"I hear Wedder's getting out," says Mrs. Collier, Darla's mom, as they watch Mrs. Wedder hurry up the street. "My cousin knew them when they lived in Milton. Says it was all an accident. With Pickle showing up drunk at odd times, something was bound to happen. He got there, that last time, at the crack of dawn, just as Wedder was going hunting. There was a scuffle and that was that. Diane still has the notion that her dad would have been a country star."

Geneva watches until Mrs. Wedder turns and disappears onto Harley Street, where Patty and Carol will be coming out of St. Cecilia's with visions of Jesus still hanging from the cross.

Darla grabs Geneva's hand and together they jive and twirl on the sidewalk and sing Bill Haley's tune but refrain from showing their Sunday panties.

Geneva first sees Mr. Wedder at the Royal Hotel on the following Tuesday, after school. Geneva and Darla order orange crush floats as they slide into a booth. Others join with demands for shakes and fries and flapper pie, all bubbling like carbonated energy uncapped at the end of a school day. Buddy Holly is spinning in the juke box, singing "Peggy Sue."

"That's him," whispers Patty Schultz. "Diane's dad."

"You mean step-dad," says Carol Simmons.

Geneva looks over to the counter. Mr. Wedder is sandy-haired and scrawny, engrossed in his soup.

"She's taking off, but don't say anything," says Carol.

Diane and Carol, both in grade nine, collude on things Geneva can't fathom. "With him?" she asks.

"Are you crazy?" Carol smirks and whispers something to Patty. Both girls are wearing black eyeliner now, looking more and more like Diane. "She's going to be a singer. And she's going to get a guitar." The two of them giggle. "Diane the Pickle performing with Elvis the Pelvis." Patty Schultz coughs and sputters, choking on her coke.

It occurs to Geneva that Diane Wedder—or Pickle, whatever her name is—has been out of sight the last few days. "Is she sick?"

"Who?"

"Diane."

"Like I said"—Carol shoots another glance at Mr. Wedder as she leans forward and lowers her voice—"she's going away.

In fact, don't you dare say anything, but she left today."

On Wednesday, after school, the girls have almost reached the hotel when a cruiser pulls up in front of the RCMP detachment. In the passenger seat sits Diane Wedder with her eyes fixed on the dashboard. A crowd of school kids gathers while Diane is led inside.

"They can't make her do anything," pronounces Carol. The crowd falls into two different grooves: the restless ones, mostly boys, jostle and tease each other under the spell of an impending event, while the others, like Geneva, Darla, and Mary, huddle and whisper. They are all waiting to see what will happen. Soon enough Mr. and Mrs. Wedder hurry up the street, like celebrities trying to avoid the public glare, and disappear into the office of the RCMP. The venetians are closed tight. Store owners watch from their front doors, seniors lean forward on benches, and young mothers push their baby carriages across the street—all curious but keeping their distance.

"She's done it this time," says Patty Schultz and no one argues. The door finally opens and the Wedders inch down the stairs. The crowd, suddenly subdued, pretends to look the other way until Diane puts an imaginary mic to her mouth and belts out her song.

There's a burst of laughter—even Mrs. Wedder's mouth forms a half smile—and Mr. Wedder waves his arm high above his head, his acknowledgment to anonymous fans. They walk toward Harley Street with Diane in tow. She puts her hands on her hips and wiggles her bum at the crowd. Geneva and Darla roll their eyes but are enthralled as well.

By Friday the word is out. The Wedders have run off without paying rent; they've run out of town without a word about where they went. The girls congregate along Neville, outside Mary Stewart's door. Carol Simmons says she knows *something*, but she isn't telling. Darla repeats her mother's story about how Mrs. Wedder was broke and Mr. Wedder couldn't find a job and the bank was no help. Mary Stewart retaliates, saying that Darla's mother is a busybody; Mrs. Stewart explained this long ago. Patty Schultz maintains that Diane is going to be a famous singer and will be able to buy her own house.

Geneva looks upward and spies a baby robin teetering on the edge of its nest. It fluffs its new feathers and lifts its wings as two other heads bob from inside. Mom and Pop banter nearby while sounds from the ground, from Geneva's gaggle of friends, fade away. Geneva watches spellbound until the baby totters back into the nest, but for sure it will try again another time.

Here's Looking at You

❦

IT'S SEPTEMBER, before Geneva's thirteenth birthday. Martin Fry walks into Roberts Hardware, veers past Geneva as she dusts Royal Albert cream and sugars, and goes right up to the glass-covered cabinet full of expensive knives. Geneva's father is out delivering an electric heater. Her mother stands behind the counter and stiffens her back when Martin walks in. "Is there something you're looking for?" asks Mrs. Roberts. She doesn't sound at all like she wants to make a sale.

"How much?" he says, pointing to a fish knife.

"Those are expensive."

"How much?"

"I'd have to look it up," she says, then finally pulls out a price list, traces her finger downward, and announces, "Fourteen ninety-five."

Martin walks toward Geneva's mother then stares right past her at the boxes of Imperials and Canucks and Whiz Bangs, stacked like the cartons of cigarettes in Lee's Grocery Store. He stands there, his broad back to Geneva, arms hanging uncommonly still. He doesn't say another word. Then he turns abruptly and walks down the aisle. Floor boards creak; rope and cable, axes and saws, and bins of nails jangle; islands of china and glassware rattle. Martin bolts out the door, leaving static in his wake.

Geneva has never encountered Martin before. He was born the year the town of Bradshaw planted Northwest poplars along the residential section of Main Street. By the time she was born, right at the end of the war, the poplars had already formed a solid column of shade and protection in front of her house. They are part of her assumed territory, along with the caragana hedge, the Siberian crab, the open veranda, even the moon and the stars. As a child she skipped along the sentried boulevard whenever she wished, to and from the hardware store.

In hindsight people judge Martin according to their favourite theory of human behaviour. He developed, as small-town boys do, into a freewheeling explorer with few constraints beyond suppertime curfews. But in his seventh-grade picture he stands in the back row, looking like he could lift bales much more easily than the gangly farm boys could. His complexion is pale and his smile is ironic, like he is sharing an inside joke, yet his eyes are intense and estranged from others.

At the time Martin was considered a regular boy who was mainly drawn to car engines and gopher hunting. He hung out at Ralph's Motors—so often you might have thought he was Ralph's son (his own father was missing in France)—and tracked home engine grease into Emily Fry's spotless house. Like other boys he carried buckets of water to nearby stubble fields to flood gophers out of their holes and whack them dead. When he turned twelve he used a .22 rifle to shoot them instead, before cutting off their tails. The difference between Martin and other boys was that he always did this alone, always in private, before taking his booty into Roberts Hardware for pocket money, a penny a tail.

Mr. Roberts collected the tails in tins and shipped them off to Fish and Wildlife for compensation. His mucking with cars and gophers rankled Emily Fry, who complained to both Ralph and Geneva's father as if they were to blame for Martin's pastimes. That her son was a loner was irrelevant.

All this Geneva has learned by listening to adults reminisce and try to make sense of Martin Fry's life. That her father kept collections of gopher tails is the bigger revelation.

"That guy's up to no good," says Geneva's mother.

"How would you know?" says Geneva who has begun contradicting her mother, turning cheeky, even though Martin Fry gives her the willies.

"He's back from Ponoka," says Mrs. Roberts, as if this explains it all.

"So? Aunt Terry and Uncle Bill live in Ponoka." Geneva is baiting now. She knows exactly what her mother means. They sometimes drive to the grounds of the mental hospital on Ponoka's outskirts to admire the gardens. No one mentions that they might also see the patients, yet once they enter the grand circular driveway they invariably grow silent as if conversation will instigate some mad uprising.

The hospital has its own water tower and power plant with groves of trees planted here and there. Geraniums and shrubs front the brick anterior while a plotted garden and fields of hay can be seen at the back. It is a large estate with its residents seemingly mute. The most Geneva has ever heard above the hum of her parents' Ford Fairlane is a magpie bragging or a robin scolding. The inside, she surmises, is hushed and sterile. She pictures the men and women in their separate wings, secretly watching through wire meshed windows, as Martin Fry might have done, though now he would be on the outside looking in.

Geneva's father has returned to the store, and Martin is peering in the window, his nose not quite touching the thick pane of glass.

"He was in here looking at knives and gun shells," Mrs. Roberts says to her husband. "And he had a strange look about him. Maybe we should talk to Pierce."

No one in town calls Danny Pierce constable or officer or anything like that. He's twenty-three, a neophyte and new to Bradshaw, and is therefore an object of curiosity and skepticism. Corporal Jensen is, as everyone knows, on vacation in Vegas, so Pierce has been left in charge.

Geneva often watches Pierce slip on his regulation hat as

he goes down the steps of the RCMP detachment, right across the street from the hardware store, and into the Royal Hotel. Aside from the coffee shop (she rarely sees Pierce there), most of the hotel remains uncharted territory. She sometimes waits outside the beer parlour with her friend Darla, inhaling whiffs of beer and cigarette smoke while Darla summons her parents for money and permission to go to the Roxy.

Geneva intends to tell Darla how Martin Fry has been staking out Roberts Hardware and how Pierce could come to the rescue if Martin gets out of hand. She'll leave out the part where Pierce falls in love with her, since Darla would be hoping for the same.

In *Gigi,* the town's prevailing picture show, Maurice Chevalier sings "Thank Heaven for Little Girls," and then Louis Jourdan, as confirmed bachelor Gaston, sings about what a fool he's been not to have seen that the much younger Gigi, groomed by aunts to be some rich man's mistress, has grown up before his eyes. Suddenly he realizes he's in love and marries her. Geneva imagines herself with Pierce; she pictures him waiting for her to turn sixteen and eventually walking down the aisle in a silk gown and flounced veil with all of Bradshaw watching.

"I'll deal with him," Geneva's father says to her mother. "You go over and tell Pierce."

"If he sees me over there he'll put two and two together and blame me if he gets caught and sent back."

"I'll go," says Geneva. "He won't notice me. I'll talk to Pierce while you keep Martin busy."

Her parents look at each other and mull the idea over. "Okay," says Mr. Roberts. "If Martin comes in I'll distract him while you slip over to the office. Be discreet."

"I will." If she could, Geneva would go directly to the phone. *Darla, you won't believe what's happening.*

"You just keep dusting over there until he has his back to you. Don't let him notice you."

Just then Martin walks in, straight down the aisle, straight to the counter where Geneva's parents are waiting. He didn't acknowledge Geneva earlier, and this time is no different. *Does he know I exist?* He nods at Mr. Roberts.

"Hello Martin."

Martin stares at the stacks of gun shells behind the counter. "What do you recommend?"

"Depends on what you want them for." Geneva's father looks over Martin's shoulder, raises his eyebrows, and gives her the go-ahead look. For a moment she freezes (Martin could turn and actually look at her), but then she slips out the door, turns right to be out of view, crosses at the intersection (people only jaywalk in Bradshaw), and walks toward the office of the RCMP.

Through the door's window she sees Pierce with his cropped sandy hair, feet up on an oak desk, talking on the phone. Potent energy percolates through his fingers as he taps the desktop and flips a pencil from one digit to another. He smiles into the receiver and then, when he happens to look toward Geneva, his eyes widen and his feet slide to the floor. He motions to her to enter.

"Okay. Gotta go. Ditto. Bye," he says then turns to Geneva, his smile fading. "So, what can I do for you?"

"Uh, it's Martin Fry.... My dad wanted me to tell you ... he's in the store right now, Martin is, and he's looking at knives and gun shells and my parents want you to know."

"You're the Roberts girl?"

Her face flushes. *Who else would I be?* She nods at Pierce and replies, "From the hardware." Now she's angry. Maybe those questions about Pierce's competence have some basis in fact. "And my name's Geneva!"

"Well, Geneva Roberts, I'll have to make a note of this." Pierce enters something into a log book, then goes over and peers through the venetian blinds. Martin Fry is just coming out onto Main Street. "I see he's left the store. I'll talk to your dad."

"They don't want Martin to know I've come over."

"Mum's the word."

"They don't want Martin to know he's being reported, in case it backfires."

"It'll be taken care of," says Pierce in a serious tone, unlike the one he used earlier, when he was on the phone, when his voice was soft and musical. "So how old are you, Geneva?"

She considers explaining that she's *almost thirteen* but replies, "Thirteen."

"Hmm." He smiles vaguely as he looks her over.

The song "Gigi" plays in her head.

"Thanks, Geneva. I'll see you around."

So this is how it goes? Her stomach flutters. *See you around?*

There is a faded quarter moon. The flank of poplars outside the Roberts' house wore flashy green-and-yellow uniforms in daylight and then darkened, as evening progressed, into rogue footmen. A figure, under one expansive tree, stands aligned with the gnarled trunk, arms hanging uncommonly still.

The smell of liver infiltrates every room of the Roberts' house. There's no escaping this weekly dose of butchered iron prescribed and cooked by Geneva's mother in a frying pan with butter and onions and a sprinkling of salt. The smell has fanned out from the new electric stove to the dining and living room at the front of the house and the bedrooms along the side. Geneva, with legs draped over the back of a kitchen chair and head and shoulders down on the seat, is on the phone with Darla. "I was right there in his office. He asked me how old I was ... and he's going to keep an eye on us, watch out for Martin Fry. Ooh, he gives me the willies. So, you want to go to the show on Saturday?"

Mr. Roberts is reading *Ellery Queen* in his green easy chair, and Mrs. Roberts is ironing sheets while listening to Frank Sinatra on the radio.

"Will you close the curtains and blinds, dear?" says Geneva's mother. "By the way, Gladys Hartley wants you to babysit Saturday night. Call her tomorrow, just to be sure."

"But I was planning to go to the show with Darla." Geneva stands at the picture window, staring at the Northwest poplars. One of them, the third one from the end, the most abundant one, seems different.

"It's still *Gigi*. And you've already seen it twice."

"But I want to go again before it changes." Her voice trails off.

"What're you looking at?" her mother asks.

"Nothing, I guess." She yanks the cord so the curtains swish together.

"Maybe I shouldn't be alone, with just a baby, in someone else's house. You know, with Martin Fry around." She moves to close the venetians on the side windows.

"The police will take care of Martin. Your dad talked to Pierce and he'll handle it."

"Maybe we should lock the doors."

"If it would make you feel better." Mrs. Roberts sets the iron on its end while Frank Sinatra sings a Gershwin tune about wanting to be watched over. Mr. Roberts keeps right on reading while Mrs. Roberts goes to the front door, turns the barely used lock, and then lifts one corner of the lace panel to take a peek. She immediately screams her head off.

Mr. Roberts drops his *Ellery Queen* and runs over to her. "What in heaven's name...?" Geneva stands frozen, her hands to her mouth.

"He's out there. His face was right up to the window, looking right at me. Oh my God, lock the back door, call Pierce."

Frank continues singing about someone who carries a key to his heart.

"Turn that damn radio off," says Geneva's father as he hustles to the back door and locks it up. He calls the operator. "Get me the RCMP. What do you mean he's not there?" Eva Shantz, the operator, knows how to reach everyone in town. Between her rubbernecking and people treating her like an answering service, she has the goods on most everyone. "Yes, it's important, dammit. Why else would I be calling?

Well put me through to the hotel then, if that's where he is."

Geneva is almost in shock, but not to the point of missing this tidbit on the whereabouts of Danny Pierce.

Her father mutters, "Why would he be there, just when we need him?"

Her mother answers, "I heard he's got a love nest."

Then he's back on the line. "Hello. Hello Pierce. We've got problems with Martin Fry. He's looking in our windows. God knows what he's up to. You gotta come and get him. Well *get* some backup! I don't give a damn who you get, just get over here."

"Next thing you know he'll have her pregnant," says Mrs. Roberts.

Love nest? Pregnant? Geneva stares at her parents.

"He'd better get here soon," says Mrs. Roberts. "Martin must know we reported him. He must have seen Pierce come over to talk to you. That damn Pierce! Oh my God, close all the windows. What about the basement?"

"Calm down."

"I am calm. I am calmly thinking of all the possibilities. And don't just stand there!"

Mr. Roberts goes around to the bedrooms and then down to the basement while Mrs. Roberts waits at the top of the stairs. "He's crazy. They never should have let him out," she natters into the stairwell.

Geneva stares at the enamelled front door. Suddenly there's a knock, hard and persistent. "Someone's at the door."

Her mother hollers down. "You'd better get up here. He's knocking at the door."

Mr. Roberts comes up out of breath; his eyes dart around the room as he gauges the situation. He goes over and pushes aside the lace curtain to face the knocker, and Geneva and her mother lean forward to see what they can see.

Martin's face is contorted; his mouth forms words they can't hear. He points toward the driveway at the side of the house.

"What? What's that you're saying? You're calling *me* a fat liar?" Geneva's father hollers through the glass; neither one can hear the other.

Martin yanks at the door and raises up his hands, exasperated. Suddenly two figures emerge from the shadows of the caraganas: one small and hunched, the other broad, bold, and in uniform. There's a thump on the door and scuffling sounds from the veranda. Voices fade and a car door slams. Then comes an officious knock and Mr. Roberts opens up.

"Okay, we've got him!" Pierce looms in the doorway. "We're driving over to Ponoka tonight," he says to Mr. Roberts. "By the way, you have a flat tire." He points to the side of the house.

Geneva and her mother rush to the front window and push aside the curtains. As Pierce opens the cruiser door and the interior lights flash on, they spot his backup, Emily Fry.

"Thank God," says Mrs. Roberts. "Poor Emily. So it's true about Pierce and Shelly Walsh?"

"Who cares?" says Geneva. "Who cares?"

Mrs. Roberts has proved prophetic. Shelly Walsh got pregnant while her husband Dennis was in Drayton Valley working on the rigs. Darla's mom said everyone knew that he was cheating on Shelly right from the start—but just the same Shelly shouldn't have gone and got pregnant. Shelly has escaped to her sister in Red Cliff, and Pierce has been transferred to Medicine Hat, which, according to Darla's mom, is a move up the totem pole and only about ten minutes from Red Cliff.

It's spring and the tulips are in bloom. The Roberts take a Sunday drive to Ponoka and invite Darla along for the ride. The girls giggle and whisper in the back seat of the Ford Fairlane and sing "Great Balls of Fire," then they all fall silent as Mr. Roberts turns into the hospital driveway.

"I wonder what room he's in," whispers Darla. "Look, there's someone watching, up on the second floor. It could be him. My mom says they shocked him with electricity, cleared out his brain, so he wouldn't recognize us anyway. Won't remember anything. Can you imagine?"

Geneva remembers the last thing Pierce said to her—"Here's looking at you, kid!"—when he stopped at the hardware to say goodbye. She can barely conjure up the faces of Martin Fry or Danny Pierce nowadays, but she can still see the look, fleeting as it was, on the face of Emily Fry: mouth pinched and curled into an ironic twist, eyes intense and estranged from everyone, including her son.

The Case

❁

BILL ACKERMAN ALWAYS CARRIES BAGGAGE: a duffle bag for hockey games, a briefcase for sales, and now a flat leather zip case. The leather case seems to go with him everywhere. He brings it to family picnics, ball games, shopping, and always on the road. Being prudent, Geneva Roberts never asks about the case.

Bill is married to Geneva's favourite aunt, the youngest of Geneva's mother's family, who is only seven years older than Geneva. When Aunt Terry married Bill, there was a big hullabaloo because, according to all the relatives, he wasn't up to par. He was her high school sweetheart, cocky, with a measure of celebrity in Bradshaw, though likely a flash in the pan elsewhere. He was handsome in the way a five-foot-nine, junior left-winger can be with a scar across his nose and another above his left eyebrow (insinuating ruggedness) and a sensual mouth advertising lust to susceptible girls. Some still have crushes on him. There is talk that he could head to the NHL in spite of his size, and even Geneva's parents won't deny the possibility. They attend games like everyone else with the duplicitous notion that success could rub off on them if the unlikely should happen.

Terry was a luminous beauty, five-foot-two and barely nineteen when she wore her princess gown, satin gloves, and hand-sewn veil. As her junior bridesmaid Geneva wore periwinkle taffeta, dyed slip-on shoes, and a band of flowers in her hair.

The outfit now hangs in a plastic bag at the back of Geneva's closet with the periwinkle shoes settled at the bottom. If she unzips the bag she can still smell Evening of Paris and inhale the promise of romance. Geneva believes people in love are bound together no matter what the others say.

Terry and Bill have had two babies since then: Denise and Jeffy. They are enthralling cousins—cuddly in Geneva's arms, chatty or coy from across the room, and flutter-bugs at her feet. She often stays over—it's almost like having a second home—and colludes with Terry on domestic dreams, sharing the ironing and the baking without her mother overseeing, and observing the embraces and groping when Bill gets home from a trip. Terry no longer follows him to out-of-town games.

He plays for the Ponoka Stampeders and sells mutual funds on the side. These are both considered to be temporary measures—Toronto or Boston, Detroit or New York, even Chicago (probably not Montreal) will be calling. He was written up in the *Red Deer Advocate* and the *Edmonton Journal* as an up-and-comer, the favourite to succeed.

Geneva's parents have driven her to Ponoka to stay with Terry for the weekend. Before they reach the house, they take a quick tour of the mental hospital grounds. Geneva's mother wants to see the place with a fresh dusting of snow—her idea of a winter wonderland. She also gives a rundown of the latest Bradshaw residents staying at the hospital: Edna Hillman, who helps her husband at the drugstore and apparently helps herself to too many powders and tablets; Inga Jensen, who should be over menopause by now but engages in girlish flirtations and has stories of young men flocking to the coffee shop because of her sex appeal, not her burgers; Angus Beamer, whose wife of fifty-one years woke up dizzy and then keeled over while cooking his bacon and eggs, sending Angus (the one with the high cholesterol) into perpetual mourning and depression; and of course Martin Fry who is still there since he harassed the town almost four years ago.

At Terry's they have dinner and talk about Martin Fry. They say he mutilated a cat just two weeks before he went into Roberts Hardware to look at knives and gun shells. Denise and Jeffy play with their meatballs and spaghetti.

"Obviously something's wrong with a guy to do a thing like that," says Geneva's father. They all agree.

"Well enjoy yourself," says Geneva's mother later as they hover at the door. "We'll be back to get you Sunday night. Don't forget to lock the doors." The door sticks when she tries to open it so Geneva's dad has to give it a yank. Then they are gone.

Geneva bathes the kids while Terry cleans the dishes—Bill is a stickler for neatness, likes everything in its place. When he goes to out-of-town games Terry lets things go, and when Geneva visits they make chocolate fudge and watch late night TV and leave the tidying until the next day, like little girls, giddy with chocolate.

Before they settle into a movie or Johnny Carson, Terry lets Geneva sample her perfume and eye makeup and puts their hair in rollers for the night while they play records (instead of listening to the game). Terry sings "Love Me Tender" along with Elvis. It's her song because Bill sang it to her when they were dating.

Geneva puts on "Travellin' Man." "Every time I hear it I think of Kenny Peterson," she says. Her face turns red. She thinks Kenny even looks like Ricky Nelson; he slicks his hair back and has the same sexy lopsided grin.

"Ooh, don't think I know Kenny."

"He's new to town." Geneva envisions living with Kenny in a rented house, just like Terry and Bill, but she doesn't mention that. Besides she might want to be an interior decorator, and that means going away to school, not to mention the fact that she and Kenny have never been on a date. Nonetheless she imagines a two-bedroom bungalow, like Bill and Terry's, which she decorates to the amazement of everyone, especially Kenny. She envisions moss green satin curtains against green-and-cream striped wallpaper, plus dark velvet cushions on a cream brocade couch. She and Kenny roll on the couch.

The next day Terry makes sure makeup and bobby pins and samples of perfume are cleared from the dresser while Geneva bounces Denise and Jeffy on the bed. Terry dusts powder off Bill's leather case. "Bill *never* leaves this behind," she says.

Geneva blurts, "Do you know what's in it?" She wishes she could take it back though because it's none of her business.

"Uh unh." Terry shakes her head. "Everyone needs to keep something for themselves. Bill says even married people should keep some things private from each other. Someday you'll understand."

"And you've never peeked?"

"No." Terry sounds unsure of herself, like maybe she should have looked.

Denise and Jeffy chant, "Daddy, Daddy!" when Bill arrives on Sunday. They clamp onto his legs as he sets his duffle bag down and tries to walk across the floor. He grabs Jeffy and swings him up onto his shoulders. Denise is frantic to have the same, but Bill grabs her by the hands and swings her back and forth into the living room. They are delirious as Bill throws them up in the air and catches them on the way down, each impatient to have their turn.

Terry manages a kiss, and Bill tells her he scored the final goal and made two assists and was picked number one star of the game. Then he hoists the children up again. Geneva watches and grins with her hand across her nervous stomach before each potential drop of a cousin, but Bill catches them every time. He looks bigger, more muscular than before.

The energy in the house finally subsides, except Bill seems to have a tic. He paces, going from room to room, maybe inspecting (Terry has tidied up), and then comes out with his case.

"You forgot it," says Terry.

"You need some milk," says Bill as he looks in the fridge, and suddenly he is out the door with his case, like the tail of a tornado, leaving eerie silence in his wake.

Terry and Geneva are speechless, and the children whine so they are put down for a nap.

Bill is gone longer than it takes to buy milk and when he comes back he is mellow. Terry is showing Geneva how to make pastry. Bill stretches on the couch and listens to Ray Charles.

"Are you okay if I have a quick bath?" says Terry. "You just slice the apples then mix in sugar and a tablespoon of flour and sprinkle with cinnamon and dabs of butter. Then roll out pastry for the top."

"Sure," says Geneva, and she quickly slips into an apple pie world, trying to cut long curly peels, slicing round and round, rolling the pastry in crisscross rhythm. The sound of the periodic furnace blast, the water swooshing in Terry's bath, and Ray Charles's voice all fade away. The kitchen is her world.

Suddenly two hands are on her waist.

"How are you doing there?" says Bill.

"Oh, you scared me!" First she freezes, then she moves closer to the counter in the little space that's left. "I'm making apple pie."

"I see that."

She feels his heat across her back. She breaks away, manoeuvres to the sink as though she needs to wash her hands and spouts whatever she can think of. "Mom and Dad are coming to get me and are staying for supper. I hope this turns out. First time for making pie. So you were the star? Good for you. I think I need Terry to help finish this off."

Bill grins. "I think you're doing fine."

She can hear the bath water draining. "Oh, I hear her coming out."

Geneva's parents come to take her home. Dinner is very good, the pie is delicious, so everyone says. "You'll make someone a good wife," says Bill and winks at Geneva.

"Not anytime soon," says her dad.

Geneva's dad asks Bill about the game. Scouts were there from St. Paul, Minnesota and have put Bill on their list.

"That's a long way from here," says Geneva.

"You'd be able to come stay with us on vacation," says Terry. "You always say you want to travel."

"Yeah," says Geneva. She glances at Bill and looks down. "Or you could come here, when Bill is on the road."

They say their goodbyes and, again, as they try to leave, the door sticks. Bill moves in and pulls hard to let them out. He is bent on fixing the door as Geneva and her parents go down the walk and get into their car. He is kicking the door as they drive away.

People in Bradshaw like to talk about Bill these days. Geneva hears them in the hardware, talking to her mom and dad. Their boy has been called to the twin city Rangers—one step closer to the Rangers in New York. They notice he's been doing more body checking in Stampeder games, clean or otherwise, which they agree you need to do to play with the big guys. So what if he's been in the penalty box more often? He's out of their league. Wait'll he gets to St. Paul. Geneva's father says very little, considering his brother-in-law is on the verge of fame.

Terry and the kids are waiting in Bradshaw; the Roberts' house is bursting with too many bodies. Bill has to find a place for them to live, other than the motel where he is staying. They wait and wait until Bill surprises everyone by arriving at suppertime on a Friday. He says he flew to Edmonton before catching the bus. His face is puffy, the rims of his eyes are red, and he looks sad, very sad, and rumpled and bulkier than before. It must be all the travelling. It hasn't been that long but Geneva thinks memories have a way of tricking you. This is the Bill that girls have a crush on?

Terry hangs onto Bill as though she needs to prevent him from leaving without her. Bill brags that he's already top of the heap in St. Paul. It's just a matter of time. Terry gazes at her star.

Geneva is excited for another reason: Kenny Peterson has asked her to the dance. She purposely hangs back when Kenny arrives at the house so he can see that the soon-to-be-famous Bill Ackerman is a part of her life. Kenny, however, is in a hurry—his buddy Ron is waiting in the car, anxious to go pick up his girlfriend who lives out on a farm.

Kenny, with one arm across Geneva's shoulders, manoeuvres the gravelled country road. With Ron on her other side Geneva feels cozy, though at times, when the tires seem to slide, she wishes Kenny would have two hands on the wheel. On the way back to town, the radio blasts "She Loves You" by the Beatles and they all sing, "Yeah, yeah, yeah." They turn into a sheltered side road, and Kenny pulls out his mickey of rye. He shares swigs with Ron and his girl. The radio is off but they still sing, "Yeah, yeah, yeah." Then Kenny draws Geneva's face close to his—Ron and his girl are busy in the back—and she tastes Kenny's Ricky Nelson lips. Not bad, in spite of the whisky breath.

The hall is packed and the Regents are playing Chubby Checker and Beatles songs. Kenny leads Geneva to the floor where backbeat inhabits her body. Newcomers arrive from out of town and command their own section of the floor, particularly a mop-haired blonde twisting her life away, skirt cut above her knees, one knee still bleeding from falling outside. Geneva can't help staring at the bloody knee as it moves back and forth to the music; it seems a dissolute knee, dancing in disgrace. Kenny also seems mesmerized. The girl stumbles again, this time to the floor, and Kenny rushes to help her up then huddles with her in front of everyone, even her date. He asks her name and says things no one else can hear. Geneva stands alone in the crowd until Kenny returns to dance with her, though he seems distracted, like he is dancing mostly with himself. When he walks Geneva to her door and offers a perfunctory kiss, she knows he's in a hurry to go somewhere else. Still, she has "Love Me Do" playing in her head.

Inside her house Geneva sees more blood. There is blood on the carpet, on bathroom towels, on a kitchen knife, and there is blood staining Bill's hand. Geneva's dad is wrapping Bill's leg, elevated on the coffee table, with a compress and gauze.

"We'll have to take him in for stitches," says Geneva's dad.

"But why, Bill? Why?" asks Terry, but she doesn't wait for an answer. Instead she heads to the bathroom to vomit her distress.

Bill mutters about a hand that was gripping his leg, a foreign hand, an evil hand that was preventing him from going places, that made him drag his leg to the kitchen for a knife. This is when Geneva's dad changes his mind and says he'll head to Ponoka. He calls a neighbour to help him along the way.

Geneva's mom cries and says Bill could end up with Martin Fry. Terry tells her sister to shut up, and they cry together.

Today the house is very still, though robins can be heard chirping outside because the screens have been installed. Bill's leather case leans against the bedside table. Terry and Geneva's mom have gone to visit him. Terry must be crazy if she hasn't looked inside—at least that's what Geneva thinks. And she'd be crazy too. She pulls the zipper, suddenly in a rush. At the bottom is a syringe, and there are papers of all sizes with Bill's handwritten messages on each. Some are poems of frozen sloughs, open and free, opposite of enclosed arenas. There is a voracious spirit yanking on doors, lured by chanting cherubs and fragrant apple pies on the inside, and the heady constraints of shoulder pads and elbow pads and knee pads strapping tight on the outside. For the first time since they took Bill away, Geneva cries.

She pulls out her periwinkle shoes and dress from the plastic bag. The waft of Evening of Paris turns her stomach; she now prefers Chanel N°5. She stands at the mirror and holds the dress under her chin. No point in trying it on. She outgrew both dress and shoes some time ago, but she still likes to see the effect of periwinkle on her hazel eyes. Tears blur everything she sees in the mirror.

Summer is finally here and Geneva is stretched out on a blanket on the lawn surveying pictures and reading snippets about Frank Lloyd Wright. It starts her thinking beyond the colour of walls and curtains and furniture. There is the evolution of the Prairie Style house, the L-Shape and the inclusion of environmental setting in architecture. She thinks of Bill and Terry's rented house, a sad comparison. She wonders where they will live when Bill gets out.

Maybe she'll be an architect. She no longer imagines Kenny Peterson in any interiors, that's for sure.

Gone

❀

GENEVA ROBERTS STARTED UNIVERSITY in September. In a perverse turn of events, her best friend Darla Collier got married, even though the two girls had planned to room together. The change of plans began when Darla's mother, Diane Collier, disappeared—suddenly gone from Bradshaw and, for all Geneva knows, from planet earth.

The disappearance inspired Geneva's mother to tell her own story.

It was a perfect August evening, over eighteen years ago; the scent of Regal lilies, Mirandy roses, and a freshly mown lawn drifted through the garden, and later, when the moon was bright, when the truth was known, droplets of diamond and ruby dew illuminated the petals and leaves and the blades of grass.

Mrs. Roberts, in shorts and maternity top, had been watering the peonies when she saw her own good friend, Muriel Spelling, walk past their house on Main. She had called out to Muriel, thinking they would have a chat, but Muriel strode past, in her all-weather coat, as though her life depended on something. Mrs. Roberts lost control of the hose; it twisted to the ground, spraying her legs and sandals with cold water, distracting her temporarily. When she looked again Muriel was gone. The hose was left running in the grass while she looked down Main. Muriel had reached the edge of town and continued to walk with steely purpose, heading south toward the golf course and the bay.

Mrs. Roberts was miffed but also unsettled, unsure of what was going on. She found out soon enough. Muriel had walked two and a half miles out of town: along a short stretch of highway, down the dirt road to the golf course, along a narrow path lined with trembling aspen and mouth puckering chokecherries to a fount of rocks on the shore, then out into the chilly water of the bay. The matter was attributed to Muriel's alcoholism, although some say a botched love affair spurred her on in the end. Muriel's husband wouldn't say.

Now, in retrospect, Geneva's mother quips, "That coat was Muriel's guarantee against getting her life back." She confides that every August the garden's aroma reminds her of Muriel and claims that on that particular evening the smell of algae wafted through the yard, temporarily subduing that of her plants. She also tells Geneva that this was just three days before Geneva was born.

There is no reason to believe that Darla's mother, Diane Collier, did such a thing or that she met with foul play. More than one person saw her head to the train station just before seven o'clock, and it wasn't to lie on the tracks. She had prepared a special dinner for Darla and Mr. Collier: roast beef and mashed potatoes with strawberry cheesecake for dessert. This in itself was unusual because Diane Collier was not known for preparing elaborate meals. She preferred spending her time curling or golfing, depending on the season, or joining Mr. Collier at the beer parlour. She also worked part-time at the post office. She was one of the first to discover the convenience of TV dinners and often convinced her husband to drive to out-of-town restaurants for Sunday buffets. Yet she cooked a Sunday dinner on a Tuesday night and then left the dishes for Darla to clean up.

The station agent verified that Diane Collier had indeed purchased a ticket for the Dayliner, headed for Edmonton. She carried a large rattan purse and an overnight bag—she had obviously left of her own free will. Ironically, since she was also a serious gossip, she inspired multiple rumours about herself. She must have known what tales could follow. Some say she was obsessed with some guy who was in town for the summer working on the highway, because she disappeared shortly after the crew moved on. Others say Diane was, for the first time in her life, on a quest to determine what her dreams should have been before she rushed into marriage, pregnant with Darla and relieved to escape the alcohol-fuelled battles of her parents. Darla, who seemed to know something about her mother's absence, was mum on the subject, and Geneva was afraid to ask.

Not only did this change the Colliers' lives forever, it also crippled the artless friendship between the two girls. Geneva and Darla had shared unexplainable fits of giggling, jabbered on the phone for hours, collaborated on plans to earn respective degrees in art history and pharmacy (underlined with the agenda of meeting more interesting guys). Geneva followed through with her plan and Darla reneged; suddenly she was headed in the opposite direction. Mr. Collier spent more time at the beer parlour, Darla more on her own, although not for very long. Chuck Henderson was the replacement. If Darla skipped school in the daytime or Mr. Collier was out on the town at night, you might see Chuck slinking out of the Collier house and down the street where he parked his parents' Dodge Desoto—a cover-up that had the neighbours talking. When wedding plans were announced, the women of the town gave their support (how else would you treat a motherless girl?). They threw a huge bridal shower and prepared food for the reception. Though Geneva was the bridesmaid, she felt sidelined not to mention uninformed that a baby was on its way.

Darla and Chuck now live in a rented one-bedroom bungalow right next door to Chuck's parents. Geneva, home for the weekend, has brought a pair of moccasins, purchased in the souvenir section of The Bay, for baby Dylan. Forget that he probably won't be walking for another year. Chuck is at work at Ralph's Motors. Darla is folding diapers, now that Dylan is asleep, and the two girls sip iced tea mixed from powder.

Geneva is compelled to say nice things. "What a cozy house.... Such a sweet baby.... His eyes are so blue, like Chuck's. What a beautiful quilt! Did Chuck's mom make it?"

The pinwheel quilt on the bed triggers thoughts of sex, how Darla must have it all the time and how Geneva is holding on by a thread of conviction—one that both girls held not that long ago—for some unknown husband, even while free love is in the air. Geneva doesn't ask Darla about her mother, about how Diane Collier missed the wedding, how she foregoes holding a grandson in her arms, tweaking him to smile, getting him to hold her finger in his grasp.

Geneva doesn't tell Darla that she sometimes studies the faces of women with crimped brown hair as she rides past them on the bus, that she sometimes sees the back of Diane Collier when she is at The Bay or Eaton's, sees her riding an escalator or going through a revolving door, though her identity is never confirmed; her face is always turned away. Geneva doesn't tell Darla that she has allotted Mrs. Collier to a shadier side of life, one that she doesn't understand.

At university, Geneva is immersed in the Italian High Renaissance where the cult of genius held sway and the idea of truth was subjective. Sprawled on her bed, in a room she shares with another small-town girl, Joanne, in Kelsey Hall, she studies her art history book. She is drawn to Titian's *Bacchanal*; she's intrigued by the uninhibited revelry of the pagan party where some carouse under the darkest shade of trees while others are redeemed by patches of golden light. On the radio Mick Jagger sings "Satisfaction," which reminds her of Quinn Munroe. There's something familiar in the voice, a boyish plea, a barely detectable wavering in the larynx, a rebellious cry for sex that triggers erotic fantasies. And Quinn Munroe has the ability to swing from gentle touch to kinetic drive; he has a wiry energy that excites her and entices her to break her prohibitions.

They met when Geneva was in grade twelve and Quinn was in first year Biology. It was at a Regents dance in Bradshaw, and his ability to manoeuvre her to exacting rhythms, his cagey grin modified by seductive whispers snared her interest. His absence, only calling on occasion, holds her captive.

She watched Ian and Sylvia at the Jubilee during Frosh week, excited by the live folk aura and by the romantic couple; Ian standing tall with his guitar and Sylvia bent like a willow toward him; their voices blending in optimistic harmony, though tempered by the melancholy of "Four Strong Winds." A transient thought—too bad Ian is committed—opposed her ideal of marriage. The Rolling Stones inspire something else: primal excitement, too hot to talk about, too hot to ignore, and requiring no commitment.

All around her, on campus, are questions about the status quo, about the integrity of big business and Americans in Vietnam, and about old-fashioned fidelity and staying virtuous. The Beatles are singing "Ticket To Ride" on the radio. Less than a year has gone by, and Geneva feels estranged from Darla and her life. Nevertheless, she is still haunted by Darla's mother, Diane Collier—would still call her Mrs. Collier if they were to meet—who for some reason bought a train ticket and disappeared.

Geneva now lives close to Quinn. All she has to do is look across the court and scan the windows of Mackenzie Hall, guessing which room he might be in. Their contact is still unpredictable but she has developed an ability to imagine a solid liaison. She picks up the phone and invites him to the Wauneita Formal—girls invite the boys.

Quinn dallies. He is reading about inorganic phosphates and asks her what kind of detergent her mother uses and explains that Mrs. Roberts could be contributing to an ecological disequilibrium, unnaturally increasing the population of some organisms and decreasing that of others. He tells Geneva to check the detergent box the next time she is home. (In residence they send their dirty laundry off to Lister Hall, job unseen.) He keeps Geneva off balance then finally accepts her invitation.

That settled, Geneva bottles her excitement for several days until the girls in Kelsey, on sixth and seventh, start a battle in the stairwell, throwing water at each other from bottles and cups. The girls on seventh escalate, filling buckets and waste cans in the showers and dousing anyone below. Geneva runs along her hallway on fifth, drawn by the shrieks and clamour and the rush of water down the stairs. Her wing erupts into action and Geneva, unmindful of Quinn, joins the others, throwing emergency packets of detergent onto the waterfall to entertain those on the floors below with bubbles and sloppy froth; phosphates slipping to ground level.

There is a faint detergent smell, two days later, when Geneva exits the elevator to the lobby dressed in a black strapless gown; it is the opposite of the frothy pink dress she wore at graduation. Her brown hair is swept up in a chignon. Quinn is waiting with a corsage of baby roses. She thinks her nose is playing tricks when suddenly she inhales a whiff of lake water, of algae thriving in a receding bay (it would be frozen over by now). She is reminded of her mother's story of Muriel Spelling's suicide. Is it an olfactory memory from the womb? People can trace memories back to prenatal existence (she read it in *Psychology Today*). She quickly sniffs the roses, declares them beautiful, and asks Quinn to pin them onto her dress where cleavage is the focus. She knows he is focused, and a wild tingle runs through her body.

They park on a street overlooking the North Saskatchewan River in the Corvair Quinn has borrowed from his roommate. It was a relief to leave. Dancing in a room of mostly strangers seemed awkward compared to the familiarity of a small-town dance. Quinn, however, feels very familiar, even with eyes closed. His hands are adept at finding vulnerable zones.

Eager mouth, sensitive ears, bare shoulders are all available to his lips. The long gown is gradually hiked, and in a fast move (Quinn's kinetic expertise) he is pushing inside her and she is agreeable, though partly in shock. "Are you mine?" he whispers and she concedes, "Yes."

Back in residence she hardly knows what to think or do. She attends to an alien mix of blood and semen, a new emanation, and she doesn't walk like she did before. She sniffs her baby roses and understands she is not a baby anymore.

Geneva believes they have a serious bond, even though it's been two weeks since she's seen Quinn. She picks up her art history book and skips ahead to the twentieth century, to Matisse's *The Joy of Life*, a modern classic bacchanal, a simple rhythmic expression of joy with clean lines and pure colour. Figures recline and embrace and frolic in the open; none are looking suspect under the darkest shade of trees. She likes this trend, this equalizing spirit, this celebration of pleasure.

On Saturday Geneva and Joanne take the bus downtown to The Bay in search of new clothes—they have been eating cafeteria food by day and delivery pizza by night. Joanne is the serious shopper. Geneva tags along, though she is mostly watching for sightings. She is now sensitized to two phantoms. While Joanne checks the racks, Geneva watches for Diane Collier *and* Quinn Munroe. She sees their backs at checkout counters, their legs disappearing around corners, their hands holding onto escalator railings. Joanne tries on stretch pants and Mondrian sweaters. Geneva waits outside the change room then wanders near the main aisle.

Suddenly she sees the real thing, one right after the other. Quinn is bustling along with a twiggy girl dressed in faded jeans and a sheepskin jacket. They are rubbing shoulders and talking fast like they have known each other for a long time. Geneva catches his eye and he nods then steers the girl away. Stunned, she clamps down on her bottom lip, real tight, and holds fast to mounting tears. Then, as if this is not enough of a whammy, she is stopped in her tracks, as she moves into Quinn's empty path, by what must be the ghost of Diane Collier. They are face to face, no getting away, except for one small thing between them. A little girl is toddling in front, eager to explore anything ahead, but Geneva stands in her way. There is instant recognition beyond knowing faces and names.

"Geneva."

"Mrs. Collier."

"Mommy, come."

Mrs. Collier scoops up the little girl. "How are you? Darla tells me you're studying art."

Geneva realizes Darla hasn't told her anything, hasn't confided a single thing, but she can figure it out. This little girl is baby Dylan's aunt, and stories of romance with the highway man are probably true. Here she is, Diane Collier, looking trim, though a little saggy under the eyes and chin. She's wearing a long coat and fur hat, like Lara in Doctor Zhivago, though she doesn't exude any smoldering passion.

The toddler wriggles, slips from her mother's grasp, and starts to run down the aisle. "Sorry I have to go. Nice seeing you, Geneva. You keep it up now."

Joanne is suddenly there as well. "Who was that?"

"Just someone from home. Lives here in the city now." She doesn't mention seeing Quinn.

"Come on. Let's go look at the fish," says Joanne, now tired of ill-fitting clothes. Geneva follows without a word. They stare at neon tetras and silver lace, marble and opalescent angelfish. Green fuzz is growing on the ceramic castle and treasure chest and creeping up the corners of the tanks. Geneva thinks of Paul Klee's paintings: *Fish Magic*, where the water is so dark that fish and plants reveal their colours in the lowest gradations of light—the more you stare the more you see—and *The Golden Fish*, large with scarlet fins and a pink flower eye, a superior fish holding sway, sending lesser fish toward the margins. Did Muriel Spelling keep her eyes open in the cold water of the bay? Did she shy away from some great golden fish, feeling belittled even in suicide?

"Ooh, it stinks. They should clean the tanks more often." Geneva's voice is wavering and shrill.

"I don't smell anything," says Joanne. "You must have a sensitive nose."

Geneva holds her breath until they get outside and run to catch a bus back to Kelsey Hall. Their footsteps are muted; tires and engines are muffled. Snow is falling in large languorous flakes, accumulating on sidewalks and cars, coats and furry hats. Low-lying clouds subdue the afternoon sun. There's strange comfort in tempered light, safety in a circumscribed view.

At night Geneva dreams of levitating; she sees colourful fish perch on tree branches, moons and stars slip into the lake below while a golden fish flies through the air, lands right on her chest, then flips back into murky water.

The next day, in her book, she studies Miro's *Dawn Perfumed By A Shower of Gold*, where breasts can also be construed as eyes, where wombs and hearts hold the same spot, where red, blue, and black tendrils confuse fish with birds, where a phallic head bone also has eyes; biomorphic forms slipped from Miro's subconscious and onto his canvas to defy logic, then showered with speckles of gold.

To Geneva this all makes surprising sense. Gone are her girlhood expectations, all replaced by compulsions of an equivocal mind and a disassembled heart. But she is looking for enchantment nonetheless.

Simon and Garfunkel are singing "A Hazy Shade of Winter" on the radio.

Vive la Révolution

❂

ONE HUNDRED AND SECOND is cordoned off for the Edmonton Klondike Parade. Geneva walked along the avenue in the early Friday morning heat, down under the cool concrete bridge, and up to this amber brick building. In the waiting room she reads *The Red and the Black*, and coincidentally it is the part where the lowly tutor and would-be priest, the proud Julien Sorel, parades through the town of Verrières, high on his horse, as part of the honour guard for the King of France. His lover, Mme. de Rênal, has manipulated the situation; she has ordered his uniform, blue with silver epaulettes and saber, to replace his priestly black and convinced her husband, the mayor, to give Julien the honour for this special occasion.

Geneva reads *The Red and the Black* to while away the time in the waiting room and to fend off the accusing eyes of pregnant hausfraus. The nurse calls her in and before you know it she is sitting on the examining table in a green paper gown.

When Dr. Schulze comes in, Geneva holds the novel to her chest so his eyes immediately focus on it. He takes it from her, cradling it in his hands like found treasure, and waxes dreamily about his own fascination, in his student days, with "*Le Rouge et le Noir* and the incurable Julien Sorel." Julien, propelled by both arrogance and insecurity, idolizes Napoleon and employs military-style tactics to achieve his ambitions, including, says Dr. Schulze, "the seduction of certain women." He wonders if she has been in the grips of such an opportunist. "Is Stendahl not relevant today?"

She considers Quinn Munroe in such a light while Dr. Schulze motions to her to lie down and slide to the bottom edge of the table. He tells her to bend her knees so that her feet settle into the stirrups. His latex fingers explore.

"It's deceitful, ya? All you need is love?" He looks up at her from the foot of the table.

She covers her eyes with the back of her hand and nods in agreement.

"I saw The Beatles play in 1960, before they made it big back in England. It was not where I would usually go, that part of the city, mind you, but my friend Gerhard talked me into it. Now you'll just feel a momentary stab, and the loop will be safe inside you." He slides a stainless-steel gizmo right to her cervix.

She winces.

"Your father called while you were out," says Geneva's roommate Joanne. "Called just to say hello then wondered why you were out so early in the morning."

Geneva usually sleeps until noon. She works nights as a hostess, just for the summer, at the Waikiki Restaurant—she wears a halter top, a polyester grass skirt, and a ring of silk flowers on her head—where the waiters make jokes in Cantonese or glare at her if she guides too many customers to another's section of the floor, and where Eddy Wong completes transactions from his bartending post in the lounge. Occasionally Eddy's girls (some Native posing as Asian) arrive in person to get instructions from Eddy. Geneva has finally clued in on the nature of the transactions, because the coat-check girls have spelled it out for her.

Geneva calls Mr. Roberts back. "Well really, Dad, if it was so early you might have woken me up."

He sounds lonely. "I was just reminiscing. Do you remember

the time I took you hunting for pheasants and we got chased by a bull?"

"Yes, I sure do," she says. Geneva's lie comes in when she explains where she has been—down, of course, along the parade route—and leaves an assumption hanging in the air. It's a coincidence that her appointment with Dr. Friedhold Schulze landed on parade day, though not at the same time. His office was along that section, right near the finish, where Klondike Kate would belt out "Hello My Baby" from a floating saloon and dance hall girls would flash their garters, doing the cancan.

When she still lived in residence, Geneva had succumbed to the horny advances of Quinn Munroe and Joanne had pressed Geneva about birth control, scolded her like a parent and then gave her Dr. Schulze's number. Recently from Hamburg, he is said to be more sympathetic, more progressive than Canadian doctors about the lives of liberated university students. She finally made it there, but it was no parade.

She puts on *La Damnation de Faust* by Hector Berlioz and lets her mind wander with the music. For some Jungian reason she recalls The Shadow who was said to have the power to cloud men's minds. Then in a flash she thinks of Quinn Munroe, who seems to have clouded hers.

She was first introduced to The Shadow back in Bradshaw with her best friend Darla Collier. The girls, then in Grade Six, were routing through the mysteries of the Colliers' basement while Darla's parents were at the beer parlour and found Mr. Collier's stack of Shadow paperbacks. The covers told the story and asked *who knows what evil lurks in the hearts of men?*

The Shadow was weird. He appeared rescuing 1930s voluptuous glamour queens, their hair curled and coifed Jean Harlow style, arched brows affecting surprise, with bright red lipstick and luscious breasts bursting out of silk lingerie. Black garters curved along thighs, holding up black hose. Shoes were irrelevant, not revealed, but you could imagine those four-inch heels. There was sometimes a suggestion of imminent torture; on one cover there was potential entrapment in metal and glass, beyond anything Geneva and Darla could imagine and maybe explaining why Mrs. Collier eventually ran away. With his arms full of a woman, so to speak, The Shadow aimed his colt .45 at the evil hordes: lawbreakers, mad scientists, and supernatural creatures, characters weirder than The Shadow himself. With the collar of his red-lined black cloak pulled across to conceal his mouth (what was he hiding?) and his eagle-beaked nose, he seemed oddly immune to their glamour-puss charms. At the time Geneva preferred Archie and Reggie and Betty and Veronica, even Jughead, with their adolescent conflicts and crushes.

Quinn Munroe, who is not weird but also a bit of a crusader, likes to talk about the evils of pollution (he's a biology major) and about American civil rights and the Vietnam War, but in reality spends more time seducing "chicks." And his mouth, impudent like Mick Jagger's, is never covered up. His hair, curly and a lighter shade of brown, is unlike the slicked-down black of The Shadow. He and The Shadow differ, and maybe Dr. Schulze is right, he and Julien Sorel jibe. And maybe Geneva is identifying with adventurous sexy women who rely on some screwball crusader or even with Quinn himself, who has the freedom to screw around. After all he got her started and now she pines for more.

She turns the radio on—Berlioz is getting heavy. *We have already reached a record 95 degrees for this parade day in July. Let's bring on The Kinks with "You Really Got Me," from the summer of '64.* She fans the air with a Klondike flyer as sweat runs down her face.

Geneva has plans to spend her night off with someone new; she resolves to forget Quinn Munroe, or at least try to. Dennis Hartman arrives early, in jeans and a black T-shirt and his Buddy Holly glasses, and waits while she has a shower. They met in Lister Hall. He approached her one day in the cafeteria and soon spilled out his plan to move to the coast to study architecture, to eventually come back and change the boring trend on the prairie landscape or stay in B.C. and incorporate expansive ocean with reclusive cedar on Vancouver Island properties. Coincidentally Geneva once thought *she* could be an architect, designing houses that cozied into the curved banks of the North Saskatchewan River. She imagined rotating variations of Frank Lloyd Wright's L-Shape on regular city lots, until she acknowledged a weakness for, in fact a dread of, mathematics. Now she studies art history, including cathedrals and coliseums, though her heart is in the residential. As the shower pulsates in rhythm, she sings "Little Boxes" along with an imaginary Pete Seeger.

She comes out, in jeans and a tunic (braless), her long hair combed and left to dry its natural wavy way. Maybe the next best thing to being an architect is sleeping with one, she thinks. *Where did that come from? And remember, Dennis intends to be an architect. Who knows if it will happen?*

They skip Klondike honky-tonk and Scott Joplin rag and go to The Umbra to listen to jazz. Dennis explains contrafaction and the flatted fifth (she doesn't understand), tells her to listen to changes in the rhythm section, and praises the trumpet player. Mostly they listen like a cool couple, sipping their beers and looking serious.

Dennis tells her they can listen to Miles Davis and Herbie Hancock back at his place, but they'll have to slip into his room quietly and play the music low as his landlady does not allow guests.

The room is tiny with a single bed and one small window. Dennis moves a pile of clothes and books off into a corner. While he sorts through his records, Geneva lays back and lets her mind wander. She envisions living with Dennis in open spaces of timber and glass and stone, overlooking the Pacific, their walls adorned with Matisse, Cézanne, Klee, and Frederick Varley—she nixes Picasso; his women, certainly without high heels, are always deconstructed. "Do you know Varley?" she says.

"I'm looking for *Kind of Blue*. Just had it here this morning."

"Green! Varley did the painting *Vera* half in green. He painted one side of Vera's face—she was his student and his mistress, did you know?—soft and sensitive, shadowed mostly in ochre and green, and the other side more assertive, in blue and taupe. Two-faced, but in a good way. He had this rationale on colours, like blue-green for spirituality and emerald green for purity. And cobalt blue for royalty and mystery. Of course he added other colours, so now who knows what it all means." Geneva tells this to the ceiling with her elbows bent, hands clasped under the back of her head.

"Christ, it's broken! My Miles Davis is cracked!"

They hear footsteps along the hallway. "Shh. Not so loud," Geneva says and starts to giggle.

"Not funny," he whispers.

"Sorry." She pulls a corner of the bedspread across her mouth, covers it like The Shadow, to stifle her giggles. "Crime does not pay," she whispers and starts in again, unable to control her amusement. She thinks about Julien Sorel, that plebian introvert who capitalizes on his lovers; first Mme. de Rênal, sweet and domestic, and now the young Mlle. Mathilde de la Mole, intelligent and independent minded. And he succeeds because of his suspicious and doubting nature and by playing hard to get.

"We could go out the window," she teases (Julien Sorel climbed a ladder and went in through his lovers' bedroom windows). They could also cuddle up until the house is quiet again, but Dennis is in a funk. They wait a short while, holding their breath, and then slink out the front door. Geneva, foreseeing anticlimax, has little more to say as Dennis drops her at her apartment door.

Geneva picks up *The Red and the Black* and continues

reading chapter thirty-one. Julien Sorel, now in the midst of his tactics to subdue Mathilde de la Mole, comes up with renewed self-control and an idea—*Frighten her!*—hatched from reading Napoleon's memoirs. He is energized by his latest solution to the challenge of possessing the haughty Mathilde: *Always keep her preoccupied with that great doubt: "Does he love me?"*

    Quinn Munroe calls out of the blue. "Do you still love me?"

    "As if I ever did."

    He laughs. "You never forget your first."

    "You have to start somewhere."

    "Are you alone?"

    "Yes?"

    "I'm coming over."

    "Oh."

    He smells of Brut, that intoxicating aftershave, and Listerine, originally a nineteenth-century surgical antiseptic and supposed cure for gonorrhea, now a promise to keep the mouth kissable—a confusing blend but inveigling just the same. He's growing a mustache and letting his hair grow long. There's something about his wiry frame and kinetic maneuvering that causes her to melt. They don't have to talk.

    Just as quickly Quinn says he has to go. The New Democratic Youth is planning a teach-in in the fall to protest Canada's complicity in the war. He really does care about her, she thinks. He's just involved in bigger things. They could live a simple life, join a commune, and then she wouldn't have to watch the suits come into the Waikiki to close a deal with Eddy Wong or make high-handed requests for the best table in the house to impress a mistress.

Chapter 32. Mathilde is pregnant. Her father, the Marquis de la Mole, is furious. Like Geneva's father he is sometimes his daughter's confidant, but this was beyond his knowledge. He planned to see Mathilde rise, through marriage, to the level of duchess, not lower herself to become the wife of a clerk, a mere servant. He contemplates getting rid of Julien; he wishes for an accidental death, considers murder or banishment from France. Instead he chooses elevation; he creates a new birthright, promises money and a position in the military. All more suitable for his daughter.

"Thank God for Dr. Schulze," says Geneva. What her father doesn't know doesn't hurt either. "Vive la révolution!"

It's Tuesday. Dennis tells Geneva to meet him in front of the Arts Building, her usual haunt during regular semesters, for an architectural tour. She takes a bus across the High Level Bridge to the south side, stares out the window at the North Saskatchewan and daydreams about Quinn Munroe.

The campus is quiet with a smattering of summer students lounging and studying on the grass.

"This is where it starts," Dennis says. "This was built in 1912. They tried to copy Cambridge and Oxford instead of designing something unique to the prairies."

"But I like this," she says. "It's what I dreamed of, expected, of a university."

"Just my point. This was nothing new."

They scrutinize the ivy-covered building made of red brick and white stone. There are carvings representing and inscribed with disciplines such as *historia*, *musica*, and *philosophia*, and a stone owl guarding the entrance that displays the university crest, *Quaecumque Vera*.

They track the other red-brick constructions that originally overlooked a grass quadrangle and end up standing before the Rutherford Library.

"Modified English Renaissance of the Wren period," Dennis says. "Mid-seventeenth century for chrissake, yet built in 1951. This is supposed to be a place that nurtures new ideas."

"But I like it," she says stubbornly. "Better than the concrete and steel and anemic brick that is taking over."

"Well, I'm not finished. I didn't say I liked the new stuff here either."

Geneva feels irritable, oppositional. She changes the subject. "I need something to drink."

They go to Tuck, a rag-tag building if ever there was one, made up of fifty years of haphazard additions and extensions, its windows thickly framed with summer ivy; it is beyond analysis, percolating with conversation and coffee, cigarette smoke, wafts of cinnamon buns, and short-order cooking.

In one corner sits Quinn Munroe and next to him, not across from him, is a sleek-haired girl with wire-rim glasses and glossy lips.

Dennis waves. Quinn nods back and the girl flutters her fingers at them.

Geneva is unsteady; she doesn't know where to turn. "You know them?" she says.

"Yeah. She was in my math class. Very smart. I mean really smart. Though I'm having my doubts, seeing her with Quinn."

"What do you mean?"

"He's a magnet. Don't know why but he breaks 'em in for others. What do you want to drink?"

"Anything cold."

Dennis steers her toward Quinn and the girl. "How's it going?"

"Hey man. Long time, no see," says Quinn. He nods at Geneva.

"Mind if we join?" says Dennis.

"Sure, sit down. We're heading out though. Just been working on some ideas for September."

The girl smiles and leans against Quinn. Geneva fixes her eyes on the girl.

"We can use your help," Quinn says to Dennis, as he and the girl get up to leave. "There's a meeting Thursday night, over at Sal's. Stop around."

Geneva claims she has a headache and tells Dennis he need not take her home. She'll rest in peace on the bus and then she'll bury herself in *The Red and the Black*, though she doesn't tell Dennis that.

"Oh my God!" says Geneva. Julien Sorel takes a pistol and shoots Mme. de Rênal, right while she is praying in church. The Marquis de la Mole had written to Mme. de Rênal, at Julien's suggestion (the fool), asking for a reference before approving the marriage to his daughter Mathilde. Mme. de Rênal wrote back and, under the duress of her priest, portrayed Julien as an opportunist, using the women of each household as a means of stepping up in the world.

Julien's opportunity to marry Mathilde is ruined. But to shoot Mme. de Rênal? Is he crazy? He is tried for murder, even though Mme. de Rênal is not dead, and he invites his own execution, says he deserves it. The French and their romantic beheadings! In spite of the fact that both his lovers work for his release, that *they* each consider suicide as a resolution, and that Julien has a brief belief that he has learned what is important in life; in spite of the presence, befitting any rock star, of fawning women at his trial, he does lose his head. Then Mathilde takes his head, kisses it *(ew)* and buries it with ceremony in the cave that Julien claimed was his place of peace and happiness, where he was least ambitious. And Mme. de Rênal dies three days later, probably from heartbreak.

The Red and the Black. Done! One thing is certain. All this dying is for the birds. Geneva will stick with the French nonetheless—for now anyway. She'll read *Madame Bovary* next; apparently scandalous in 1857 and it still might be juicy. She'll check out Flaubert's story about a woman who is bored and unhappy with middle-class life and looks for passion and love outside of marriage (she's married to some kind of doctor). This reminds Geneva of a life with Dennis, probably a boring and unhappy one.

Last semester Geneva studied the movement from Romanticism to Realism and Impressionism. She has a print in her room of Manet's *Luncheon on the Grass*: two fashionably clothed men in black and grey frock coats (1860s Parisian), and a nude woman, a bather, done in warm fleshy tones. Considered offensive at the time, critics asked *who* was for lunch. The trio contradicts this slur with a look of modern consciousness and engagement in conversation. The woman looks alert, only temporarily distracted, like she is attending to the click of a camera, but she is as free as the men, even freer, unhampered by the usual ankle length, long-sleeved dress and underpinnings of corset and petticoats and stockings, not to mention boots.

Geneva now has a personal take, a new perspective on Manet's trio and a new curiosity about a female in the background, a fourth figure coming out of the water but already covered up in a white chemise. Why is she ignored in critiques? Where does she fit in, other than for artistic balance?

Marrying Stationery

❦

DEATH IS A HARSH FORM *of escape. Witness Marriage A-la-Mode,* writes Geneva Roberts. This is her final term paper (she's an art history major), and she must finish before the day is out. She has to put wedding plans with Kevin Renfrew and stale dreams of Quinn Munroe out of her mind. Kevin slumps on the couch in her apartment, smelling of Old Spice and reading *The Godfather.* He puckers his lips to the air every so often.

There's a moral to the story when you marry for money. Geneva is reviewing William Hogarth's *Marriage A-la-Mode,* though it is hard to stay focused on Hogarth or on her chosen topic of Paintings Within Painting: Symbolism in Sequential Art. Her essay is on Hogarth's series of six paintings or engravings, which tell the story of an arranged marriage, consolidated with a pile of gold, and set on a course of infidelity, syphilis, murder, capital punishment, and suicide—so-called standard fare for eighteenth-century upper-class English and so unlike the fate of Katharine Ross in *The Graduate,* who escapes from her parents' approved and promoted wedding by running away with Dustin Hoffman. Simon and Garfunkel sing "Mrs. Robinson," but they could just as easily sing "Here's to you, Mrs. Roberts." Not that Geneva's mother would ever consider seducing Kevin. Not that Geneva would ever run away with Quinn.

"The phone!" says Kevin.

Quinn Munroe is on the line. He is all about timing. Not

long ago Geneva fantasized about wearing a full-length gown, having the full-meal deal, with Quinn at the altar and the words preconceived: *with this ring I thee wed*. Of course Quinn would have found it all too bourgeois.

"I've been thinking about us," he says. "I know I haven't called in a while." His voice turns low and nasal when he wants to seduce.

"Mm hm."

"I've been telling my buddies what you mean to me."

"Mm hm."

"Are you alone there?"

"Unh uh."

"Should I call back?"

"I'm getting married."

"Oh!"

She tries to sound like there is another reason for Quinn's call, a diversion for Kevin's sake. "So ... Kent State?"

"Yes, unbelievable.... But I guess there's no point ... if you're.... Is it anyone I know?"

"Maybe. So you're planning a rally?" She hopes Quinn picks up on the fact that Kevin is at her elbow. "Let me know if you need help, though I guess I'll be busy the next while."

"Yeah. Right."

"Okay?"

She puts down the phone, feeling it heavy in her hand.

"Who was that?" says Kevin.

"Just a friend, a guy that ... well we spent time together and, you know..."

"Hm."

Kevin, who is in first year of law school, doesn't ask more, doesn't cross-examine. It is not his style. Perhaps this also explains his decision to leave school at the end of the semester to join his father's business, Renfrew Stationery. They will expand with a second store, and then who knows? Maybe there will be more. Maybe a whole chain.

Geneva Roberts has settled for marriage and is talking simplicity: a garden wedding, a small party of guests, a mini dress, and a handpicked bouquet. She'll crown her brown hair with a ring of daisies. Kevin is agreeable; he has never given much thought to such an event, unlike Geneva and her best friend Darla, who have been planning since they were little girls. Darla managed the whole shebang four years ago, even though she was pregnant and, according to some, undeserving of the white veil and gown. Geneva, however, has taken a turn towards the casual, like John and Yoko.

The Beatles "Here, There And Everywhere" will replace Wagner's *Lohengrin*, and the service will be made up of Khalil Gibran's poetry. Geneva and Kevin will write their own vows, if they can think of what to say.

Marrying stationery seems right, in spite of Quinn Munroe. Some marry oil or cattle or even publishing, but embossed paper thrills Geneva Roberts—soon to be Geneva Renfrew. She loves the business, that is the merchandise, up front. She has always made a beeline to any store or section that displays papers, pens, and staplers, calendars, notebooks, and colourful tabs, often browsing without a purchase in mind. Now she can scan the aisles after hours and have dibs on stationery, including invitations, and can order wholesale from the catalogues.

She has started a collection of paper: rice paper, origami paper (including silver and gold foil to make crane mobiles and place cards), the finest ecru vellum for invitations (she will do India ink calligraphy for the actual wedding details and watercolour block prints on rice paper to overlap the card face), a pack of Zig Zag left over from so-called recreational weekends (Quinn was the roll expert), and strips and scraps of old wrapping paper that she can't bear to throw away. She keeps it all in a Bay box, under the bed.

The roll papers seem to be all she has to show for her relationship with Quinn. She has come to her senses about him. His wiry energy, his rusty voice, and his musky aftershave have always pulled her in. But being fixated on a regular no-show just doesn't make sense, even though the sound of his voice just instigated a cover-up when really there should be none.

"Did you know that cranes mate for life?" asks Geneva, as she begins to fold silver paper into one, intending to hang it from the lilac bushes, her essay half forgotten.

"So do magpies," says Kevin as he tries to continue with *The Godfather*.

"And they are a symbol of peace and happiness and long life."

"So are bats."

"Don't be ridiculous."

"Seriously, in China the bat is a symbol of good luck and happiness and long life too. I read it in *National Geographic*. We could cut out black bats and hang them just like we did at Halloween."

"Very funny."

Geneva contemplates the marrying-for-life idea. Her mother, Mrs. Roberts, who is indeed a lifer, is keen about the wedding and not against marrying stationery either. The Renfrews in Red Deer are bigger than the Roberts in Bradshaw, and they are providing Dom Perignon, like a sacrament, to be served immediately after the ceremony in the garden. Mrs. Roberts would like a bigger guest list though, and she really was counting on seeing Geneva walk down the aisle of St. Stephen's Anglican (and who is this Khalil Gibran?). Mr. Roberts, who is closer to Geneva's heart, is agnostic and likes to question God's existence, but Mrs. Roberts tends to think he does this just for sport. He accompanies her to the odd Sunday service just to keep her happy and in denial. Kevin's parents are Anglican too but are used to catering to their son. "That's just the way he is," they are probably saying, "but he'll come around."

Kevin indulges in oppositional humour—he has been testing his parents since he was a boy—and this suits Geneva's current sardonic state. But how romantic are bats? Couldn't he be a little more Ryan O'Neal to her Ali MacGraw? Couldn't they

have a little more *Love Story* minus the tragic death?
Of course one can be delusional about love for love's sake, she continues to write. *Considered a twentieth-century descendent of William Hogarth's sequential art, George Herriman's Krazy Kat is an example of 1930s serialized masochism. It consists of a comic strip in which Krazy Kat continues to believe that Ignatz Mouse really adores him(her) and shows it by hurling bricks at Krazy Kat (POW). Here speech balloons and an irrational series of Arizona landscapes replace the kind of background symbolism, the paintings within the paintings, used in Hogarth's work. Officer Bull Pupp completes the comic triangle; he continually chases and tries to jail Ignatz while Krazy Kat views this as an ongoing game of tag.*

"Crazy. Talk about ignoring all the signs," says Geneva.

"Huh?" says Kevin

Though some of Herriman's contemporaries associated Krazy Kat with Dada, based, I suppose, on its purely emotional and nonsensical images, I believe this comic strip, though whimsical, is a modern version of bad choices.

Geneva holds the term paper in her hands, typed on regular stock, while she waits outside Professor Bremner's door and reads his comments one more time.

58%: Not a bad go re: the decline of social comment in serial art, but your focus on love and marriage is beside the point. This is, after all, an art course. Would like to see your analysis of composition and iconography. Dada, of course, self-destructed once it became acceptable. This is not up to your usual standards. Stop by and we'll talk.

Her initial response was, "Oh shit." Her future in both art and life seemed muddy. But Dr. Bremner's comments held intriguing undercurrents. He would like to hear more of her opinions. He recognized her high standards and he wanted to talk.

She fantasized that he would be her confessor, that he would forgive her for her long-time obsession with Quinn Munroe and her pliant behavior whenever he deemed to call, forgive her for her love of paper, her fondness for material things that could lead to a dubious marriage, and forgive her for writing such an unfocused essay and for not knowing more about Dada, and for not realizing he had an interest in her. Please forgive her.

Kevin Renfrew is on the line. Not long ago Geneva fantasized about a garden wedding and a life in stationery.
"I've been thinking about us," he says.
"Mm hm."
"I've been having second thoughts. Even third and fourth ones."
"Mm hm."
"Are you alone?"
"Uh no."
"Okay. Is it someone I know?"
"Not really."
"Uh huh."
"Just so you know I have a chance to raise my final mark. I'm doing a paper on the series of eight pictures in *A Rake's Progress*. And did you know about William Hogarth's own infidelity?"
"Not really."
"Well, just so you know."

SURREAL HEARTS

Transforming Doctor Zhivago

❀

AT THE EDGE OF ANNA'S GARDEN was the small windowless shed that they never discussed; it was simply enmeshed in their daily surroundings. In fact, when she read one of Zhivago's poems in which he described her working in the garden, she noticed that he wrote about every bush and tree and building that surrounded her except this one shed. His words painted the landscape, eliminating one unsubstantiated part. The shed did not seem to exist for him, which was just what Anna wanted—at least in the beginning.

On that day Anna stroked the muslin curtain as she gazed through the window of her country cottage out to the drifting snow. Snow had wafted off the heavy branches of the willow tree and piled up around the trunk, glistening in the sunlight. Hoarfrost decorated the windowpane and, since she felt feverish, she pressed her nose, then her forehead, then each cheek, along with the palms of her hands, against the frosted glass.

Doctor Zhivago emerged from the thick pine forest in a sleigh pulled by a dappled grey stallion. A fur collar and cap framed his mustache and beard, and a fur blanket, studded with gems of ice, lay across his lap. He reined in his horse, dismounted, and walked over to the huge drift by the willow tree.

Anna's long hair rippled down her back and tickled her spine as she dropped her gown to the floor. She slipped through the glass and bounded toward the deepest layers of downy snow.

His furs had fallen in clumps around his feet as he reached

out to her and guided her further into the drift. His whiskers grazed her lips and down across her breasts.

Snow fluttered with their movements; some flakes melded one to another, creating webs of intricate designs, while others formed soft cushions or floated with the wind.

Afterward Anna helped Zhivago gather up his clothing and, since they dared not sleep in a winter storm, she slipped back through her window, trickled ice water across the wooden sill and floor, and waited to let him in through the door.

First he unhooked his horse from the sleigh and led it toward a shed for shelter for the night. There were two sheds. The one with the window had hay and straw spread around the floor for the sorrel mare that stood inside. The other was small and windowless and padlocked and apparently inaccessible, so Zhivago passed it by.

She greeted him at the door. "Will you have some hot tea?" she asked, holding out a ceramic cup. "And by the way, I am Anna."

"Thank you. It is good to be here, Anna."

A thick candle burned upon the wooden table. She could see it reflected in Zhivago's discerning eyes. The stone fireplace crackled with the remains of the midday fire. As darkness crept through the cottage, he built a new fire and the two of them sat contented, like old friends, entertained by the ravishing beauty of the flames and the impetuous music of combustion coming from the logs.

"I have prepared a table over by the window for you. You'll get the afternoon sun."

He looked over to see a table with precious paper and a pen and an oil lamp, placed there for him to write, into darkness of night if he wished. He smiled, then took his balalaika from his satchel and played for her until the fire had almost expired. After all, she had been waiting for him for a very long time.

When spring arrived, Anna tended to her garden: she hoed the weeds, carried buckets of water from the rain barrel, and thinned the patches of vegetables. In autumn she harvested onions, potatoes, turnips, and beets to make soups and stews in a simmering pot. She ground the hastily stored grains of wheat and rye, and created dark, heavy loaves of bread. Sometimes Zhivago headed into the forest and brought back a rabbit or a pheasant to roast in the fireplace; bones were later added to the pot.

In the midst of her outdoor labours, Anna often sensed him watching her through the window. Her mouth would curve into an enigmatic smile, half for herself and half for Zhivago, and then they would resume their tasks, he with his melancholy poems, she with the crumbling earth.

At night she would lie in their bed of down and watch him with his head bent over papers; sometimes he wrote feverishly and sometimes he stared out into the darkness. When he put out the oil lamp to join her they would cling together as though they were alone in the world, like Adam and Eve.

However, as time passed, the prairie earth seemed ever more demanding, begging for sustenance. Anna's bones ached and her mind seemed to evaporate along with the morning dew.

One day, after a long walk through the crumbling leaves of the forest, Zhivago returned looking expectant and hungry, as usual. Anna watched him as he approached the cottage. His face turned quizzical, and then his eyes narrowed with concern as though he sensed something had gone awry. For one thing Anna knew smoke was not spiralling up the chimney from their perpetual fire. For another, she saw that the normally padlocked shed door was flapping in the breeze. Zhivago quickened his step. A faint rumbling was coming from the shed, but still he bypassed it and hurried to the cottage.

When he crossed the threshold, Anna greeted him with her usual embrace. She directed him to his usual chair and presented him with a hot cup of tea, but he waved it away, leaving it to cool on the table. Instead of wood crackling in the fireplace there was a monotonous hum throughout the cottage.

"I have made a decision," she said. She picked up his cup of tea and walked toward a low cupboard. On the cupboard sat a shiny, metal-framed box. She opened the box and set his teacup inside. There was an insistent staccato ring. Anna opened the door of the box and again presented him with hot tea, steam rising to meet cool air.

"I hope you will understand," she said, studying his eyes for a response.

They had much to talk about that evening. Anna took Zhivago to the little shed and showed him the generator, which had been silent under lock and key and was now rumbling like the aftershock of a distant earth quake. They surveyed the wooden shelves that held other shiny boxes of various sizes, and then returned to the cottage where she tried to explain all that she had been hiding from him. She lit twigs in the fireplace and threw on some logs. She tried to put her arms around him, but he stiffened and resisted her embrace.

"You have too many secrets," he said and lurched out into the darkness.

Anna slept fitfully through the night and arose before dawn. She called her sorrel mare, hitched her to the carriage, which had been sitting unused for several months, and rode away, knowing that Zhivago had retreated into the forest.

She drove eastward across the plains. Long golden grasses undulated with the wind, the carriage wheels joggled round and round, and the sorrel's hooves clacked along the roadway, and yet a profound silence enveloped her. She travelled for most of the day, way beyond the forest, and the cottage and her garden.

He was watching from the window when she reappeared. She knew he would be. She could see his shadowy profile as she took her bundle of supplies directly to the shed. Then, still holding one parcel, she walked toward the cottage, entered, looked right into his eyes, smiled a crooked smile, and then took her parcel over to the chrome box.

"Please sit at the table," she said and clasped his shoulder. "I will prepare your meal."

The chrome box began to hum and beep, and in no time she removed a plate of steaming food and set it in front of him.

"Linguini and clam sauce. Please give it a try." She stroked his hand as if to brush away his reticence.

In the days that followed, Anna watched Zhivago progress from microwave cooking to internet browsing. He watched television game shows and Masterpiece Theatre and modern warfare on the news. He appeared baffled and incredulous, then suddenly ravenous for new experiences. Anna fed them to him at his will and watched him turn from introspective musings to computer jargon and talk show sentimentality.

"To think," he said, "that we can share our minds and souls with so many."

"Windows in and windows out and windows on the world," he wrote.

"Hockey is contained and orderly, limited in time and space, unlike the chaos of revolution," he observed.

Anna began to linger at her window again, but the winter hoarfrost brought nothing but a chill to her bones. This time she could not conjure up a fever and slip through the glass as she had done before.

As for Zhivago, he could no longer write poetry.

Then, one April morning, a warm breeze blew through the window and rustled the flimsy bedside curtains while a chorus of nightingales called from the willow tree. Anna looked out to see her mare frisking in the pasture while Zhivago's dappled grey stallion followed closely behind. Her fever erupted as it had done over a year before, at first without her awareness, then with great urgency. She knew what she must do.

She slipped through the windowpane, head and hands first, and raced toward the pasture. She called and her mare came, unbridled and whinnying. She pulled herself onto the mare's back and gripped the tawny mane. Together they leapt over the weathered log fence and travelled south for most of the day. Then they headed toward a rise of black hills that were crowned with the crimson shards of the retiring sun. Anna urged the horse into a full gallop.

Even as the sun disappeared altogether, as the hills blended with a darkened sky and teased of their nonexistence, she knew she would never return. She'd see what was up ahead.

Shifting

❄

"**Y**OU HAVE TO DO SOMETHING with your life," says Kristine's mother, perturbed that she has agreed to leave her daughter behind. "You can't drop out over every little thing. And for heaven's sake cut your hair."

With that Kristine's parents drive away, joining the exodus of cottagers heading back to school or work in nearby towns or further on in Edmonton or Calgary.

The beach is now smooth and naked. No gulls. No people. Kristine steps out of her shoes and walks across the dry sand and into the chilly water. The waves flap around the bottom of her pants and, as she moves in deeper, slap her thighs in rhythm. She turns once to see that a magpie has arrived and is watching from the shore, then she leans back in mock slumber, impervious to the cold and mesmerized by the waves, lost in thought.

You can't float forever. You must either sink or swim. Sink or swim. Sink or swim.

She hears the muffled honking of a lone goose somewhere overhead. Then a voice.

"Hello. Hello there. Are you all right?"

She lifts her head, then splashes and scrambles to stand up. "Oh yes. I'm ... I'm fine." She is shivering beyond control.

A woman stands at the edge of the water. She is wearing a long white sweater over a black flowing skirt. In her arms she cradles a blue bundle. Her face pales against the sand and her teased blonde hair catches fragments of sunlight; something seems to sparkle there.

"Guess you think I'm kind of crazy," says Kristine; her clothes are dripping and heavy as she walks out of the water.

There is movement and a gurgling sound coming from within the woman's bundle. "It's Andy," she explains. "Just three months old but he's very attuned—my nature boy already. I bring him down here most every morning to listen to the water. Sometimes we even hear the pike surfacing, though you have to listen very hard."

Kristine nods as she tries to wrap her arms around herself.

"Come on up to my cottage. I have a nice fire going. You need to get warm. By the way, my name is Nora."

Kristine follows Nora and Andy down a narrow pathway through the poplars. There is a tinkling sound, wind chimes in the breeze, then a raucous bird calling through the tree tops.

Old trees form a screen across the front of the cottage, but young saplings crop up at the back. Dead leaves rattle around the base of the trunks. A magpie, dressed smartly in a black-and-white western fringe, flies overhead calling *Watch watch watch* before perching on the red brick chimney.

Nora opens the screen door, but Kristine stands outside, afraid to go in and muddy up the kitchen.

"Oh, come on in. I'll get you some towels and something to change into."

Kristine drips water across the linoleum and then moves onto the braided rug in front of the coal and wood stove. She tries her best to dry herself, clothes and all.

"Here, put this on." Nora hands her a terry gown.

"Thank you, Nora." She shivers, in spite of the wafts of heat, removes her wet clothes from under the gown, and then introduces herself. "I'm Kristine. Kristine Welkes. I don't think I've seen you here before."

For the first time she notices the long, dangling earrings and various chains around Nora's neck and the two rings in the side of one nostril. She does not want to be caught studying the nose rings so her eyes settle on the silver chains.

Nora's pale, skinny arms and long delicate fingers begin to flutter over the stove as she stirs a huge black pot of soup with a long wooden spoon. Nearby, on a wooden shelf, are jars of spices. The jars at one end contain some very unusual looking ingredients: dark, dried up, indecipherable globs of matter.

Outside the window a pair of magpies banter and jockey across the woodpile. *Witch witch witch, witch witch,* they say.

"Here, have some soup. It's my very own recipe. It'll warm you up and calm you down. It even keeps Andy peaceful when I eat it; my milk is so good for him."

Kristine sits at the table and inhales the spicy aroma. Andy is indeed a child of mellow disposition; she has yet to hear him cry. She takes a sip. It's an unusual taste, pleasant enough, but obviously laced with a unique combination of herbs and spices. The flavour, though intense at first, quickly dissipates, inducing her to take another spoonful and another and another.

"Well, now that you have colour in your face, I can give you a little advice. You really need to be looking to the sky, not the water for your animal. I see you following the air currents. Just watch for tornadoes, that's all."

"Pardon me?"

"Now Andy has a real affinity for the water. His animal will be from the water. But you, you need to look up."

"Uh, I like the water, and I hate heights."

"Yes, I know."

"And what do you mean look for my animal?"

"It's your link."

"Link to what?"

Nora gazes at her with no apparent intent to reply.

Without warning Kristine begins to laugh. "I'm feeling soporific. Know what I mean? Ha ha. Soporific."

"Lie down on the couch. There's an afghan for a cover."

"Yes, I think I will if you don't mind. You've been really kind." She pulls a blue afghan over herself.

Her change in form is unaccountable. She begins to soften and dilute and flow in rivulets, yet her thoughts remain intact. She rolls and glides and drifts and wanders in oceanic splendour. She joins the stratosphere. She *is* the stratosphere!

Then she develops rigid edges that stream out horizontally to form a plane, and she understands the terrible burden of holding the earth in place.

Magpie sails upon her surface. He is light and aerobatic, like a kite in the breeze, and while she holds him afloat, he begins to dart up and down through various stratums. Suddenly she's like the tail of a kite, following him through his comedic escapades.

She shrieks then gasps as they light upon a fir tree.

"How's that for a ride?" he says, and calls out *Rich rich rich, rich rich.*

They glide over to the red brick chimney and teeter on its edge. He flashes his iridescent blue tail. Until now she thought magpies were strictly black and white.

She looks down to see a girl, about four years old, sitting in a pile of sand. The child's blonde curls reflect streaks of sunlight while she digs in the sand with a worn metal shovel. She sprinkles the white crystals along her legs, her thighs, and onto her dimpled knees. She rakes her fingers through the sand and lifts out old root fibres and cigarette butts, discarding them helter skelter. She seems mesmerized by the piling on of sand, and soon she is blanketed from waist to toes, leaving the tender skin of her upper body open to the breeze, the mosquitoes, and the soft slanting sunlight.

The little girl leans back, forcing her toes to thrust out, and reveals painted crimson nails that wriggle and flash in the sunlight. In the instant that Kristine spots these nails, Magpie takes her on a fast glide down and waddles toward the girl in a cocky, self-assured manner. With his fine pincher beak, he attempts to extract a crimson wriggler for himself.

"No, don't!" the little girl cries, flinging sand in their direction. Magpie backtracks and squeals while he raises his wings and jerks his neck forward for one last try, but the girl begins kicking her feet and more handfuls of sand explode and spray across his wings and along his illustrious tail.

Magpie screeches and scolds. *Wretch wretch wretch wretch wretch.* He moves to the grassy edges of the sand pile.

"What is going on?" cries the mother to the little girl as she bursts through the screen door of the cottage.

"He's after my toes. He's trying to bite my toes." Tears stream down the girl's face.

Magpie pulls Kristine into the shadowy south side of the cottage, and then they dart up toward the rippling warmth of the tree tops.

The mother heaves a rock, which ricochets amongst gnarled old poplars and green saplings, creating a tune of pops and riffles.

As they settle on a top branch, Kristine asks between breaths, "Why did you do that?"

"Because I saw the wrigglers there. I wanted them."

"But you actually bit her toe. You hurt her, frightened her. It's only nail polish, you know. Not wrigglers."

"She flashed those wrigglers right at me so I went for them. What can I say?"

Below them the mother cries in a fury. "I'll get you, you pesky magpie. Just try that again and I'll give you something to remember me by. I'll fix you." She takes the girl back into the cottage.

Roach roach roach, cries Magpie, getting the final say.

"*Bitch bitch bitch*," Kristine hollers along with Magpie and begins to laugh out across the tree tops while rolling with the breeze.

She settles on the branch of a tall poplar and looks down toward the cottage, again aware of her fear of heights. "Oh my God, this is high!" Then she spots Magpie. He has gone back down without her. He surveys the ground again, walking across the sand and the grass and then up along the railing of the cottage verandah. There is a sandwich on the table.

Catch catch catch, catch catch, he calls.

Another magpie replies, *Watch watch watch, watch watch.*

Kristine spots Magpie's mate in her black-and-white finery, calling from across the road, right next to a ball-shaped cluster of twigs. A young magpie, with a soft puffy breast and a short black tail, is clinging to a branch below.

Magpie ignores the warning and struts across the table toward the sandwich. *Catch catch catch*, he calls.

Suddenly the cottage door is flung open and the mother yells, "I told you, get the hell out of here!" She has a newspaper in her hand, rolled up like a baton, and she screams with a rage that reverberates through the trees and over the water. She flails at Magpie and sends him careening across the table and fluttering at the edge.

"Fly out!" Kristine screams just as Magpie attempts to fly. But the woman manages to thwart his balance and knocks him to the floor. She crouches over him. Her dark hair flies across her face, across the ugly contortions of her mouth and eyes. She slams the baton down, over and over and over again.

Magpie squeals, then wails, then moans and sputters.

His mate cries frantically from across the road, then lands next to Kristine, sending an outpouring of desperate pleas. She rants and dives through the air. Kristine can only cling to the branches as she trembles with fright and anger.

The woman grabs Magpie's tail and flings him into the bushes. "I warned you," she hollers as she slams the cottage door.

In an instant of resolve, Kristine sails down into the bushes, crashing through rose hips and saskatoon saplings. Magpie is on his back, on a bed of dainty white clover. She reaches out to him, with her now clearly defined hands, and lifts him gently up on her knees and strokes his fine white breast, feeling the warmth within. His heart beats, though very faintly.

"Oh please.... So sorry, so sorry, so sorry."

She awakens to hear Andy wailing and sobbing while tears stream down her own face.

"Are you okay?" asks Nora.

"No, I'm not. I'm not okay. What have you done here?"

"Here, take Andy for me." Nora speaks quietly and offers Andy.

Kristine scowls but sits upright on the couch. She takes Andy in her arms and holds him close. She caresses his head against her shoulder and rocks him back and forth. His crying gradually stops, then he shudders, his energy all spent. The two are melded in a peaceful aftermath.

"I'll take him now," says Nora.

But Kristine continues to cling.

Nora pulls him gently away and holds him to her breast.

The wind chimes call and Kristine looks for glimpses of the lake. "I'll be going now," she says.

"I know," says Nora. "There's a beaver down there. He's Andy's, so you'll watch for him, won't you? They don't often come to big lakes, you know."

Gentle waves move toward the inlet. The reflected sunlight shimmers across the water, occasionally stopping at small islands of weeds. Near the beach are poplars with barren tops that exude a golden glow. Across the lake, along the horizon, are gentle hills with patches of black and ochre.

Kristine moves to the waters edge, aware of another's presence. She sees him slink through the water, his slicked-down brown back surfacing in unpredictable locations.

"Hey, I'm Andy's friend," she calls, then throws off the gown, Nora's gown, and runs and skips through the water. She dives in, gliding and surfacing and gliding again as though Magpie is pulling her along. The beaver seems unafraid as he pops up here and there with a quizzical look in his eyes.

Over on the shore she spots a fluffy young short-tailed magpie, looking forlorn, attempting to fly on his own at the grassy edge. "Hey, there is something that you should know," she yells. "You can either fly or swim!" She maintains, of course, one eye on the water, the other on infinite sky. "Hey, wait for me. I have something to tell you."

Flight 2100

❀

ALICE HAMILTON CHECKS THE DOORS and the windows. She checks them again and then sits in her rocker and looks out across the temperate South Saskatchewan River and up to the crystalline sky. A jet stream is shooting up higher and higher. She contemplates the solid white ribbon that suddenly breaks and disappears somewhere over the prairies. She imagines a heavenly ballet of hadada ibis wings fluttering over the river, then closes her eyes and begins to dream of giraffes aspiring to the tops of acacia, or loping across the savannah, their heads held high with royal grace. An eerie taunt from a spotted hyena interjects and causes her to jump in her chair. Gradually she realizes it is her doorbell. "Just when I was on my way," she cries. Her bones creak as she lifts herself out of her chair and heads to the door, convinced that she should be dead by now.

"Oh, it's you. I was just dozing a little. Come in. Can I get you some tea?"

"You know, in Spain," she continues as she puts the kettle on, "they always have their siesta. And bull fights! Now there's something I refused to see. Come sit down. There's that story, you know, *Death in The Afternoon*. Archie fancied he'd be like Hemingway; he insisted on going and I said fine, but you'll go without me. And he did. Damn him anyway. Pardon my French. Now he's done it again."

Archie promised to be there, to hold her hand while *she* drifted away. She left the details to him, the itinerary so to speak, which is just the opposite of her usual tendency to obsess over dates and times and travel gear. She believes in heaven and all that, and she's certain that it's her destination—she's baptized and confirmed; she's received her confirmation for flight 2100.

Archie was always the travel instigator. They'd get offers and brochures in the mail, and then he'd quickly decide that they would go to Istanbul or Kenya or Peking or the Galapagos. These were package deals, so the arrangements were relatively uncomplicated. But first he had to persuade Alice, then he had to let her talk through it, worry over it, fuss a little. This was not the same as worrying *about* something. Alice did that compulsively. This was an unspoken ritual. She would line up the reasons for not going; he would counter them. If he hadn't played along she would have been in a quandary, left to answer her own protests, and possibly reject the trips altogether. They would have stayed home. She would not have a house full of art objects from around the world, she would not be able to regale friends with exotic stories of Masai warriors guarding their huts at night, or steamboats taking them down the Amazon with savage piranhas lurking in the water, and that deadly imitator of coral snakes, the micrurus, slithering in the nearby rain forest. She would not be able to sit in her blue rocker with her blue eyes closed and picture the giant icebergs of Greenland floating by.

But Alice finally made it clear that they were too old for this business of taking off to other countries, and she meant business. It was hard to keep up with the other travellers, and, truth be told, it was hard to even leave the house. This was different from her standard worry routine, and Archie seemed to understand the certainty in her voice. "You'll have to go without me. I'm finished with all that." This, of course, was not what she really meant, the part about him going without her. Their lives had been thoroughly intertwined for fifty years. Their comings and goings were mapped out on a course that even the finest traffic controllers wouldn't alter. The shock was that Archie actually did leave without her.

She didn't see it coming, didn't really listen. After fifty years she knew, better than anyone, what Archie was about, but things slipped by her anyway. For instance, he complained about shoulder pain. That was easily explained. He had broken his collarbone after falling from the ladder. He had insisted on pruning the Manitoba maple himself—he didn't listen to everything she dictated. He showed signs of recognizing his limitations: taking afternoon naps, hiring a school boy to cut the grass, turning down invitations to anything that ran too far into the evening.

When the grandchildren came to visit, he didn't turn down the usual wrestling on the carpet or trampling along the South Saskatchewan, but he cleverly redirected the children's energy, engaged in mild deceptions, not unlike the ones Alice had used throughout her life. He did a lot of talking, a lot of kidding around the periphery of their activities, to make it seem like he was part of the action.

"Oh, you got me!" He faked defeat from his arm chair. "And he jabs a left. He hooks with a right," he commentated for his grandson. "Oh, she has me trapped. I'll never get away," he called out in a boyish whine. "Help me, Grandma!" he teased as his granddaughter pulled on his arm and his neck and his shirt, whatever she could grab, to draw him further into their play.

Alice knew what was going on; at least that's what she'd thought at the time. She could hear the rabble rousing from her kitchen, and she would holler at him to be more careful as though Archie were a kid himself. When he complained of sharp pains, she said it served him right. Take a little aspirin, have a good rest. What did he expect at his age? Of course he had pain in his shoulder and even down to his chest. Of course he should be tired out. Who did he think he was? At his age?

Then, goddammit (pardon the French), he left without her. At first it seemed like a hoax, one of his silly practical jokes. Forget the invasion of urgent young men carrying a stretcher through her door. Archie was really just lingering in the zucchini patch, poking around their terraced gardens, hiding in the underbrush of willows and red dogwood and high bush cranberries. Or out on one of his jaunts down main street: into the Royal Bank, along the fronts of his commercial properties, over to Rogers Coffee Shop, into City Hall for the latest gossip on aldermanic shenanigans, then into Winnies Toys with grandchildren on his mind. At any moment he could barge in the door waving some red-tongued rubber cobra or neon dragon kite, and she could lecture him about spoiling those kids.

Just yesterday the ladies covered her dining table with a finely woven brocade from Florence and laid out tea and coffee and dainty sandwiches and dessert squares baked by the Anglican Ladies Aid. Her guests carried silver-rimmed china plates to plush chairs or cedar lawn furniture—they are no longer of an age to stand around and mingle and flow from one group to another. They had the choice of teacups with saucers or coffee mugs, the latter being Archie's preference, Alice's too. In her mother's day a mug would have been out of the question on such an occasion, but times have changed, and she likes being practical, or, as she still says to others, *they* like being practical. She tends to speak for both of them.

Archie used to explain to her, to his son and daughter-in-law, to guests that would listen, that he had everything in order and, with a crazy grin, that he was ready for flight 2100.

"Oh, don't be so silly," she would say, or, "No one wants to hear about that. Now when we went to China...." And then, "No, I wouldn't want to change my life for all the tea in China," or "Remember that song? Come along and be my China doll? Okay, okay, it was party doll." She had heard it years ago it on her son's record player. She had a way of moving through a conversation by association of words. You didn't know where it would end.

Today the table is cleared except for the china. The ladies

washed it all by hand and stacked the saucers, four at a time, topped by four cups nestled sideways. "We brought a doll back for our granddaughter from China, made of papier maché, ha ha. No china doll from China. Actually, we brought an Anne of Green Gables doll with a china head from Prince Edward Island and a porcelain figurine of Marie Antoinette from France. Archie wanted to bring back this cake plate with Marie's head smiling from the center. His idea of a souvenir. But you know there's no one like the English for making dishes. My mother grew up near the porcelain factory in Worcester, and we still have pieces that she brought over with her. Now I'm more partial to earthenware than bone china, but you know, at times like this it's expected." She shrugs and hands her visitor a mug of tea. "Did you know they use ashes from animal bones? That's why they call it bone china. A kind of cremation and recycling. My brother insists on being cremated, when the time comes, but I don't know...." She shakes her head. "Says we use up too much land with cemeteries. I suppose he's right. They make some very nice urns you know—beautiful plain or multiglazed earthenware—and I'm sure they come in fancy bone china as well."

"Pardon me? Oh no, they wouldn't *make* the urns with people's ashes, they use the urns to hold the ashes. Oh no. Goodness me."

"It is the strangest thing," Alice explains. Whenever she walks from the living room ("What if it was called the dying room?" her son had once taunted as a boy) to the kitchen, she passes the corridor that leads to the oak-panelled study on one side and the red powder room opposite, then turns right to the bedrooms and a bathroom. Just out of the corner of her eye, she catches Archie going around the corner, perhaps out of the study. She always intends to get a cup of tea just for herself, but then she gets his mug as well, the large ceramic one, the one with *Number One Grandpa* printed in old English letters. She fills it to just the right level. She knows by sight just how much space to leave for two and a half teaspoons of sugar and enough milk to turn the tea to light beige. "Would you like some tea with your milk? That's what I always say." But his cup just sits there and gets cold, and milk forms a ring inside the mug.

"Stupid," she says of herself. "Damn him anyway."

Smile

❃

Be happy while you're living, for you're a long time dead.
—Scottish Proverb

THE FIRST TIME SHARON THOMPSON saw him he looked just right. Just as he should. Not exactly like her father, but something about him was akin to her father, something reincarnate. It was the smile. They had the same turned-up corners of the mouth and eventually the same blue-grey eyes and sandy hair.

Mother and son bonded immediately. She named him Dewey, meaning beloved, after scouring a book of names. Babies first present a social smile around four to six weeks. Any earlier and it is attributed to gas. But Dewey was an exception. He often seemed to be amused, to have a real sense of humour, as soon as he was brought home. He was precocious in this regard.

Dewey would never know his grandfather since he was born three years after Alec Thompson died. Sharon, in perpetual mourning, slept with Dewey's father, Derek, as a means of feeling close to another human being. They parted "on good terms." Sharon was determined to avoid a marriage that might end up like the one that her parents, Alec and Agnes, had. For Dewey this meant growing up with a single mom and having occasional visits with an out-of-town dad who had moved to Toronto to pursue a career in soccer but ended up selling commercial property instead.

When Dewey turned fifteen Sharon decided he needed a male presence, and Derek, his father, agreed. She put Dewey on a plane to Toronto for the summer holiday.

Dewey, who is not athletic, has been forced to play soccer with his dad and swim lengths at "the club." For some reason that even Sharon can't fathom, she fixates on the club. "What's with this club you go to?"
"Keeps me from being scunnered I guess," says Dewey.
"Scunnered?" Sharon hears him grinning over the phone.
"Yeah. Bored. Don't you know? And guid words cost neathing."
She is amused by his Scottish accent. It distracts her from her concerns. It wasn't easy letting go, even though she was convinced that Dewey needed his father. "Okay, smarty. I hope you're having fun."
Part of Dewey's fun at home has been collecting *Spider-Man* and *Punisher* and *X-Men* comics. Maybe he is still amused by them and is also stacking them up in Derek's condo, sliding them into plastic covers, reticent to share with careless hands. Secretly Sharon considers Dewey a nerd. But that could be a good thing. Boys like him come into their own later than the norm, often in a big way. It is uncanny, though, how he has developed this other voice.
When into the sauce her father, Alec, often slipped into a working-class brogue, a Glaswegian accent that was much thicker than his own. It was like he adopted a second voice in order to dish dissent about his wife. "Aye, the lovely Agnes says to me in so many words, 'Yer oot yer face,' and you know what I says to her? 'Ah dinnae ken what yer sayin'. Drives her mad." His state of mind inevitably morphed into melancholy, which was spurred on by headaches and retching, not to mention the resultant shame and remorse. Though he never articulated these feelings, they were palpable as he downed aspirin with pots of tea, especially in the face of

Agnes's fury. Sharon sided with her father when her mother seemed on the attack.

Alec had his own business, Thompson Insurance, but liked to say that there was no real insurance in life, as if he mocked his own line of work and enjoyed the irony. In retrospect Sharon admits that her father was at times morose as he plodded through the day-to-day requirements of life. He was successful in his own small way, admired in the community, but his bouts of drinking filled in unexplained gaps and probably began with a buzz of sociability on special occasions such as Christmas and New Years and Remembrance and Dominion Day. Still, she was his favoured child and she favoured him back.

Then Alec died. Sharon's mother, Agnes, had, by a stroke of luck, a black pillbox creation with a little black veil to screen the eyes. It was a perfect fit for Sharon, and Agnes insisted she wear it to the funeral. Sharon tried to rebel, to let her hair cascade down her back and go to the service hatless. Her father would have understood, even found a way to commend her decision, but she gave in under the strain of losing him. Really, what did it matter? In the end she put her hair in a chignon, and the veil created a refuge, a distance from those who came to grieve, not to mention a curious disembodiment, a feeling most surreal.

Agnes had become a milliner just when hats were going out of style. Sophie's Hats and Things was a short-lived shop in town. Before Sophie moved on she befriended Agnes Thompson, as she befriended many others, hoping to create a bank of devoted customers. Agnes was bitten by the creative bug itself and became more interested in making hats than wearing them. She convinced Sophie to share her expertise. This also coincided with her first reading of *The House of Mirth* and her fascination with the impossible Lily Bart, who did a stint as a milliner instead of marrying for money.

Though Agnes had been married for all those years, she could still imagine herself starting over. She worked out of her home and made what she called mad money from friends and acquaintances. Now with Alec gone she stocks supplies and does her millinery anywhere in the house. She has created an otherworldly air, draping boas and capes and fanciful hats on mannequins. When Dewey visited as a young boy, he challenged the mostly female apparitions to duels and galactic wars. Agnes made him costumes worthy of Luke Skywalker and Darth Vader. Now boxes of felt and straw and netting are stacked up in the master bedroom. Feathers, artificial flowers, crystal embellishments, bands and combs, stiffeners and dyes cover the vanity, while finished creations sit on wooden blocks along the wall. She mainly sells white veils for weddings and black-veiled hats for funerals.

Dewey calls Sharon on a Saturday. "A roukie afternoon," he reports. He and Derek have done their lengths at the club. "You won't believe this, Mom. You really won't. Keep the heid now."

"Okay. What's up?"

"We were looking at old photos of the club members. And who do you think was there?"

"Dewey, just tell me. I can't possibly guess."

"I'll give you a hint."

"Fine."

"He's a deid man. Someone near yer hert."

"What are you talking about?"

"Grandad was a member of the swim club. 1945."

"Dad never lived in Toronto."

"Oh, yes he did. You should come see for yourself. Seein's believin a' the world ower."

"Okay, Dewey, please stop the Scottish shtick. What makes you think it's him?"

"I checked the records—date and place of birth for Alec Thompson. Looks like all the other early pictures of him. Ask Grandma."

"All right, but I'm sure you have the wrong man."

"Deid men dae nae herm," says Dewey in his deepest voice.
"What? Let me talk to your dad."
"He's oot. Oot and aboot."
"Okay, stop Dewey. Just stop."
"All right, all right."
"Get your dad to call me, will you?"
"Sure, but he's probably on an all-nighter."
"He leaves you on your own?"
"I'm fine. I'm not a little kid anymore. By the way he's in pictures with this other woman."
"Your dad has his own life."
"No, I mean Grandad. Has his arm around her, sitting cheek to cheek."

Derek calls her on Sunday. "A dull morning here," he says.
"I'll just bet," she replies then wants to take it back. Derek's love life is none of her business, but it does affect their son. "So ... you leave Dewey on his own?"
"Okay, Sharon. He's not a baby anymore, and I'm not about to treat him like one."
She wants to ask about the club, about Dewey's new way of talking. Is he on something? Do father and son get high together? Derek was into that when he was younger. She wants to ask these things, but she is afraid to insult the two in their father-son bonding. Afraid to be labelled a smothering mother.
"So, has he met any new friends?"
"Well, I think he's got a crush. There's this girl at the club that he hangs out with. Penny."

November is a mild month. Some years they were deep in snow by this time, but this year the land is dry. They had a brief snowfall in late October, before the deciduous leaves (except the poplars) had a chance to turn to red or gold or crispy brown. Instead the frost turned them into an eerie loden green. Red apples turned copper and now hang from branches like ornaments at Christmas, shining in the afternoon sun. Grass is still green.

Agnes is vague about Alec's stint in Toronto. At the same time she confirms it. "He was rejected for military service because of his flat feet, so he thought about studying law. We took a break, that's all."

Dewey and Penny are internet sweethearts and texting fanatics. When Dewey announces that Penny will be coming to town, Sharon is alarmed. He is already neglecting school. "She's coming to visit a cousin," Dewey says, but Sharon knows better. She saw a message that he forgot to close. *My bonnie Penelope I'm mad with it. On the electric soup my lass. Can't wait to feel yer ass.* It's a combination of young nerd and testosterone. Sharon isn't sure if Dewey is all talk, if Dewey is experimenting, or specifically if Penny has led him into dicey territory. Penny is, after all, older.

Sharon, to prevent the two from being idle, has made plans. She got them passes to the wave pool, tickets to *David Copperfield*, to *A Christmas Carol* and to The Tragically Hip. She would never have tolerated this interference from Agnes, but then maybe she wouldn't have gotten pregnant either. What she has not anticipated is Penny's obsession with Agnes. The girl even hangs out at Agnes's house without Dewey.

Penny loves to try on all the hats. She throws on wispy scarves and filmy gowns and swirls around the house to "Danse Macabre." "Call me Penelope," she calls out, and Agnes is both flummoxed and flattered by it all.

"Isn't she something?" asks Agnes when Sharon arrives, like an intruder, in the middle of Penny's dervish.

Sharon can only purse her lips and roll her eyes in disbelief. "She is something," she replies.

Agnes's old Motorola is now in full use blasting forties nostalgia. Alec was the one who had collected all the records. Now Penny seems a devoted student of the era. No rock 'n' roll for her. They listen to Bing Crosby croon "Only Forever" and, since Christmas is coming, "White Christmas." There are the big bands: Glenn Miller with "In The Mood" and Harry James with "You Made Me Love You." Lena Horne torches "Stormy Weather," and Frank Sinatra sings "People Will Say We're In Love." Penny seems more nostalgic than Agnes.

Dewey prefers Radiohead and Tea Party and Metallica and Derek's old Beatles collection. He seems out of Penny's loop. It is straining their connection. Sharon is really not sorry to see them head in that direction. But there is Sharon's mother. Penny has captivated Agnes. Or is it the other way around?

Dewey, seeming perplexed, often paces around the house. He gets irritable over the smallest of things, and then, most unlikely of all, he targets his grandmother. He corners Agnes on an afternoon when Penny is out with her cousin for a change. Agnes is pinning French netting to form a white veil at the back of a black satin pillbox. "It's for Penelope," she explains.

"I can't tell if it's for a wedding or a funeral," says Dewey. "By the way why was Grandad living in Toronto when you were already married?"

"Well, dear, sometimes, you know, people aren't certain about the decisions they make, and sometimes they take a break just to see how they feel."

"All right. Did you take a break before or after he was seeing someone else?"

"Dewey! What has gotten into you?"

"Seriously. I need to know."

"But why?"

"I just do that's all. It's chawing me. Sorry, Grandma. I don't mean to bother you."

"Chawing? Where are these words coming from?"

"I don't know. I'm not myself. Ever since Penny."

"Penelope is a lovely girl, don't you think?"

"They have the same name, Grandma. That woman in Toronto. The one I saw in the picture with Grandad. I thought it was a happy coincidence, but now I'm not so sure."

"Dewey. Now listen to me. Does your mother know about this?"

"Just that he's in a photograph with another woman."

"Okay. Good. Let's keep it that way."

"And they look like more than friends."

"But Sharon doesn't know her name is Penelope, right?"

"Right."

"Dewey, we are going to clear this up once and for all."

Agnes decides on Frank Sinatra.

"Yer as daft as yer day's auld," says Dewey in a baritone voice quite unlike his own.

"Never mind," says Agnes.

"Naething like bein stark deid," says Dewey.

"Speak for yourself."

"Deid men are free men."

"Then be free and let Dewey go. Oh look, Penelope is coming."

"She leuks like butter wadna melt in her mou."

"You sound like you're on the sauce."

"Wad that I coud."

"You should have taken care of this in the first place. But you never were decisive," says Agnes.

"Crabbit. Yer no to be made a sang about."

"Oh quick, put on Sinatra," says Agnes. "Ah, Penelope, we were just talking about you. I've made you a hat, dear." It is the black pillbox with the white French netting flowing at the back.

"It's a confused hat," says Dewey.

"Oh no, dear. This is the new vogue." She places it on Penny's head. "What do you think, Penny? Dewey? Let me take a picture," says Agnes. "Okay, smile."

Frank Sinatra sings "I'll Never Smile Again."

Agnes has copies of the photo printed for everyone, even Derek. Penny and Dewey face the camera without showing a single inclination to touch one another. Penny is wearing the equivocal pillbox and Dewey is wearing new red-lensed glasses and a knit beanie, looking like a young Bono. They are an odd couple, and for some reason Penny has begun to fade.

Much to Sharon's relief Dewey has moved on to a Calgary girl who has a penchant for newsboy caps. Agnes says she is not capable of making such a hat.

Saving Britannica

❀

DENISE LEANS SIDEWAYS ON THE BACK of the olive sofa and peers through the blinds, but she ducks whenever a car drives by. She does not want to be caught just watching and waiting. The sun is setting behind the houses across the way, creating halos over the rooftops and boomerang reflections off windows. If you were walking by you wouldn't see in her window anyway, but her habit is ingrained. It has been so since she was a little girl waiting for her father to arrive. Waiting to surprise him as he opened the door, back from his sales tour of neighbouring towns and, if he was lucky, with orders for the entire revised fourteenth edition of the Encyclopaedia Britannica.

"Red or white?" asks Sheryl.

"Either one is fine," says Denise as she turns to face her sister. "What do you feel like?"

"I found this merlot in the porch stash. Not bad considering Mom's tastes." Sheryl already has the bottle in one hand and a corkscrew in the other, like she has anticipated her older sister's indecisiveness.

Denise lays a volume on the cushion next to her.

"It's all online now, you know," says Sheryl. "It's a bit like Wikipedia, except Britannica still controls sources."

"I know."

"I've seen sets on eBay for over a thousand," says Sheryl.

"I know."

"We could easily sell."

The corner bookcase stands floor-to-ceiling next to the window, and a maroon leather club chair is in front of it. All twenty-four volumes of the Britannica still sit there along with Book of the Month Club hardcovers, and even though the chair is arranged with a standing lamp for cozy reading, Denise wants to sit on the floor behind the chair and randomly pull out volumes and open pages to surprise herself with new information. She wants to do this while natural light slips away with the absurd notion that no one will know she is there. This too was so when she was a little girl.

Sheryl was just a toddler when he left. Eleven years between the girls, Sheryl was a surprise. She says she has no memory of their father. No sentimental attachments. Vern was her dad for all intents and purposes. He was the one who taught her to skate and paid for her education and walked her down the aisle.

Vern, it seemed to Denise, had achieved unwarranted legendary status when he died. Sheryl and their mother Alice were in mutual mourning for at least a year. Denise grew tired of it all and wondered at how her mother had let Vern into their lives so quickly.

The bookcase is the way it has always been. Rarely has a book been added in forty years, and it has gathered a lot of dust in the two months since Alice died. Sheryl has no interest in housekeeping. It is still up in the air as to how long she will stay here. The state of her marriage will determine that, but eventually the sisters will sell. Denise doubts Sheryl will give up life in her gated community. Denise left married life a long time ago.

A stack of unopened mail is on the end table. Denise pushes it away to make room for her mother's crystal wine glass, bought by her father at Jamison's Hardware as a last-minute Christmas gift. Sheryl would not know any of this.

"So what's with all this mail? Are you not planning to open it?" says Denise.

"I can't bring myself for some reason."

"But some of it may be important. Things need to be attended to and stopped, and people should be informed."

"Don't mind if you do."

Stimulus and response is in motion. Wine in Denise's mouth brings on relaxation even though it has not yet affected her brain. She picks up the pile of letters. "Well, some of this is junk and can be tossed right away."

"So toss it."

"Whatever you say, madam," says Denise

The first envelope lands right at Sheryl's feet. The second one grazes her hair.

"Hey, watch it." Sheryl sends an envelope flying back.

It lands in Denise's lap just as she is taking a sip. Wine splatters onto her jeans, and a mouthful spurts onto her ivory sweater.

Requests for donations, renewal notices, fall promotions, all become missiles around the room. "All junk!" says Denise.

"Okay, okay." Sheryl puts up her hands in self defense and can't stop laughing.

"By the way, I'll take the crystal," says Denise as she sets her wine glass down.

"Fine, take all the books too. I don't know why Mom kept them all these years. She always complained about the dust, and Dad and I weren't interested."

"You mean Vern."

"Yes, Dad!" says Sheryl emphatically.

Denise tries to imagine the Britannica volumes in some stranger's hands. She can't decide which would be worse, ownership by a sister who disregards her real father or by a stranger who would not care one whit about the bond it created between a father and daughter. Denise knows you couldn't pay Sheryl to keep the books. She also knows she has no room for them in her apartment.

"Maybe we should sort all the old photos," says Denise.

"Okay. How about some music? Your records are still here,"

says Sheryl. "Moody Blues. I remember you playing this. Over and over and over." She holds up a single forty-five.

Denise barely hears Sheryl. She is already turning pages. There are four photo albums, carefully posted with pictures of Alice and Vern and Sheryl and Denise. Sheryl always seems to be entertaining whoever holds the camera. Denise tends to lean away. All other pictures are in boxes, keeping company with the dust bunnies that have infiltrated the cardboard. Many of these pictures are black and white. Alice had not bothered to put them in albums in pre-Vern times.

Denise flicks her hand and knocks her glass of wine with the sudden burst of the song "Go Now." You could say this is her song.

"Oh shit. Have you got a cloth?" More red wine stains her sweater and drips off the end table. "I just can't win today."

"You should soak your sweater right away," says Sheryl as she dabs it with a tea towel.

"I guess I don't care about this sweater any more. At least I didn't break the glass. At least it didn't spill on the pictures."

"Suit yourself."

Denise cannot help herself and sings "Go Now", along with The Moody Blues

Alice had ordered him to go. She had that stone-cold expression, that firmness of voice that Denise and later Sheryl learned to heed. And then the only one in all the world who Denise would rely on, the one who seemed to adore her and understand her, just walked out the door. Trolling the Encyclopaedia Britannica for items that her father might not know, hoping to stump him, to engage and impress him remained her habit long after he was gone. It became part of their imaginary dialogue and later transferred to her relationships with men. She wanted her intelligence to shine above all else.

"More Moody Blues," says Sheryl as she holds up the album *Days of Future Passed*. "Seems appropriate." The album cover is abstract art with a pink hourglass shaped island amidst inky blue underworld waters.

"Not right now," says Denise. "Can we just have some quiet for a while?"

"Okay?"

Denise thinks Sheryl is always agitating and impulsive, though others call her refreshing. The sisters have colluded over the years in order to oppose their mother. Now that Alice is gone, where will it go?

"I thought maybe a little music would cheer you up. Maybe even get you to crack a smile."

"Guess that shows what you know."

"I thought they were a favourite. I thought you liked them."

"Yes. Doesn't mean I always wanted to party."

"So, you liked to drown yourself in melancholy? Now that I think of it, yes, you did."

Denise turns to look out the window again. There is comfort in watching and waiting. Call it melancholy, if you will. There he is, coming down the front sidewalk in his black overcoat and plaid wool scarf. He is not your typical salesman. Circumspect and intelligent, he is a good listener and never seems to proselytize—if he was made to sell anything it would have to be knowledge. He is successful to be sure.

A sip of merlot and the voice of her sister bring Denise back to reality: her father is a phantom tied to the projections of an adoring daughter. Denise is a psychologist. She knows very well that life is sorted in the head, not the house. It is clarified in relationships with others, not in the pages of encyclopedic facts. But what about Alice? She was always here. There is no image of her approaching the house. Will she linger somewhere inside? If the house is sold, how will anyone ever know?

"Did you know that Mrs. Harris has collected over a thousand butterfly pins and ornaments and teacups? She came by yesterday to see if Mom had anything we might not want," says Sheryl.

"Lepidopteran?" says Denise.

"Huh?"

Denise begins to turn pages then reads parts aloud. "Order lepidoptera. Any more than 155,000 species of butterflies, moths, and skippers. What the hell are skippers? Many members ... especially butterflies have appealed to the human imagination for thousands of years ... have inspired the designs of jewelry, ornaments, and textiles..."

"Okay? So Mrs. Harris isn't crazy?"

"Says Aristotle gave the butterfly the name psyche, Greek for soul ... blah blah.... They may be the souls of the dead ... uh and often appear to announce the final exit from the body."

"Weird. So should we give her Mom's butterfly teacups? We can't keep all this stuff," says Sheryl.

"More wine please," says Denise.

"Do you believe in a soul?" asks Sheryl as she refills both glasses two-thirds up. She does not lose a drop. An expert is she.

"I believe in the mind, obviously, or I wouldn't do what I do. Is there transcendental energy or immortal existence or simply a combination of conscious and unconscious electrical activities in the brain? I do not know."

"So do you miss being married?"

"What's that got to do with anything?"

"I don't know. Just thought I would ask."

"I see we are into serious philosophy."

"Well, it is serious. I mean, it worked out for Mom and Vern. They were happy the second time around, don't you think?"

"You're wondering if you might find more happiness with someone else?"

"Do you think?"

"You are uncertain."

"Yes, dammit. It's why I asked. Don't talk to me like I'm your client."

"Okay. I'll have to think about that. Do I miss being married?"

"Oh God," says Sheryl. Why don't you look it up in one

of your books? Well, while you think about it I'm putting on Blondie." She puts on "Heart of Glass" and turns the volume up. She puts one hand on her hip and sings along. Her hips sway and knees bend, opposite shoulders dip in rhythm as she walks the floor; all economical and trance-like movements remembered from another time. She picks up the tea towel and swishes it gently back and forth, mimicking Debbie Harry's contained sexuality.

Denise smiles. She can't help herself. Her little sister the butterfly, the life of the family, except there is no longer anyone else around to applaud. "Go ahead, give Mrs. Harris the china. I can live with that."

"What? Can't hear you."

Denise sees Sheryl at thirteen, the up-and-comer of small-town figure skaters. She is a natural, floating along the boards, her baby blue skirt fluttering along slender thighs. She is a force of energy, an *élan vital*. Yet her focus disappears. Escaping Alice to so-called freedom was really just a switch of allegiance to boys. Denise knows this from experience with her own daughters. Insert divorce and partners with opposing views and you magnify the possibility for rebellion. She could remind Sheryl of this. Her two, daughter and son, are still in the throes of adolescence.

Alice and Vern adored every performance on ice and imagined Sheryl's future in some magical arena of renown. They never vocalized this, even to each other, but you could see it on their faces. There is still a glass-covered frame on the wall that holds all of Sheryl's medals.

Denise waves her hand and shakes her head as if to say never mind. At least she doesn't have to answer any questions. But a question does occur to her. Is there already someone else for Sheryl? She turns to her window again to see that her father is still there. He is a dim light in the evening darkness. He carries a leather briefcase. She is anxious to learn what it holds inside. He will have something for her. He always does. There is a knock on the door. "Why is he knocking?" She stops herself from thinking out loud. "Turn it down," she says.

"What?"

She moves. "Someone is at the door." She opens it to see a stranger, a man slightly younger than herself. He is tall and blond with a beard and mustache. Not at all like her father. But his eyes do sparkle.

"Hi. I'm here to see Sheryl. You must be Denise."

"Oh, I was about to tell you," says Sheryl. She has turned off the music and is right at the door. "This is Mark," she says. "I was going to tell you, Denise," she repeats. Her hand caresses his shoulder then slips into his hand. "Come," she says. "Let me take your coat and I'll pour you a glass."

Denise cradles her own glass and rubs the wine stains on her sweater. "A small accident," she explains as Mark passes through to the kitchen with Sheryl. She closes the third volume of Britannica on the sofa and waits for an end to the muffled voices in the kitchen and a return to the living room.

"Did I tell you that Mark is a realtor?"

"Uh, did you tell me that Mark exists?"

"All right. Fair enough. I was just going to."

"Well," says Mark as he looks around, "so this is where you've been hiding. The house I've been hearing about. Cozy. Solid enough. Maybe could use a little staging, but I think it has appeal."

"You can check it out more tomorrow," says Sheryl. "You don't mind do you Denise?"

Denise considers her meaning. Does she mind if Mark stays over? Does she mind if Mark inhabits their personal space and the space of her father and mother and even Vern? Does she mind if he calculates the value of her family's existence? Does she mind if he fucks her sister within earshot, in her mother's bedroom? "Sure, go ahead. If that's what you want to do?"

"Well, it's your choice too."

"Not one I was aware of until now."

"Sorry. I was going to talk to you about it but time slipped away on me. Maybe we should pick up another bottle, Mark. Give Denise a little time. The Barrel is still open. We can get there before it closes if we hurry."

The house is still. Quiet as a chapel. Denise begins to sing under her breath. Sheryl has already set out the butterfly china on the dining table, destined for Mrs. Harris. What else is in store with those two?

Denise has made up her mind. At the same time, she begins to panic. She wedges the front door to stay open, opens the trunk of her car, and in stages loads the volumes of Britannica willy nilly along with some familiar old titles. She is breathless when she hears a siren. It feels like she is committing a crime.

She knows who the local police are. She knows they have come to her door. She knows very well that loading her books into her trunk is not an offence, but she wavers in the doorway just the same, ready to be chastised; it reminds her of facing Alice in times gone by, uncertain of accusations in the making.

"May we come in?" they say.

She brushes the stains on her sweater. "Just had a little spill," she says.

In turn the officers explain in careful tones the shocking news to her. Sheryl was the driver. She had probably not expected a delivery truck coming out of the alley at that time of night, just before she would be turning onto Main Street. She was apparently in a hurry.

Mark was lucky. He could just walk away, which he did. Their spouses were spared insinuating stories, and merlot was never mentioned.

The Encyclopaedia Britannica has been returned to its rightful place in the corner bookshelf, and whenever Denise comes to her house, mostly on weekends, she sits on the sofa while she enjoys a glass of wine and turns to look out the window to see who might still be there. She watches out the corner of her eye in every room of the house to determine the appropriate spot for each one in her family. The butterfly china is back in the cabinet, and she especially watches there.

She recently read that the typical encyclopedia owner of the eighties opened the books just once or twice a year. She has surpassed that hundreds of times over.

Special Occasions

❊

HELEN MALTBY LIVED FOR SPECIAL OCCASIONS. I met her at one of these. It was at my Uncle Alvie's eightieth birthday party where grey heads predominated and jokes about Alvie living with aids—hearing aids, nursing aids, Rolaids and Band-Aids—made the old folks laugh. I sat with the band of younger relatives near the bar. Most in our group looked like they were hit in the face with a lemon cream pie when they heard such jokes. I didn't think it was all that bad.

To be honest I have never quite fit in with my cousins. Several of them, divorced and relegated to second-rate condos with bedrooms duplicated for the time share of their children, went on and on about their trips to Cuba or Costa Rica, about the quality of Australian wine and Canadian brie, and the merits of their running or fitness clubs. They still think they're the cat's meow. I was born a century too late; I would have married back then and lived a good and honest life.

Helen was married to Uncle Alvie's best friend, Charlie Maltby. This was a second marriage for Helen and Charlie, since their first spouses died about twenty years ago. This gave Helen a whole new set of occasions to attend.

Everyone marvelled at her spunk and determination to have fun that afternoon at Uncle Alvie's party. She did the Charleston once she got the band to play the right music, and we said we hoped to be just like her someday, if we should live that long. As if being old and the partying sort were automatically at odds. It crossed my mind that maybe they should be.

Helen joined us at our table and participated in one of those typical conversations that inspire people to exclaim, "Isn't it a small world!" and to shake their heads in disbelief that they both know so and so who is the stepmother of so and so (in this case me) who happens to live just two doors down from…. Well, you get the idea. I lived just two doors down from the Maltbys, although I hadn't met them until Uncle Alvie's party. This is why I got to know them more after the do.

Helen had three children and nine grandchildren. I know this because each time I visited her she asked me to go over the newest additions to her photo albums. She was chief recorder of main events: birthdays, anniversaries, holidays, and visits, but not so much funerals. There were pictures of her family with gifts opened and held up as inventory for the camera, people arranged in groups for proof of their attendance, flowers delivered and snapped by Helen's camera as evidence of their arrival, and shots of Christmas trees with multicoloured lights that obscured the individual ornaments. I think the ornaments would have told a story of their own, if I could just see what they were, but that's my sentimental nature coming out. I tend to think such things are chosen for symbolic meaning. I'm not close to my family, in fact I'd just as soon forget about them most of the time, but I *knew* Helen's children and what they might like, even though I hadn't met them.

I imagined how Helen's children would decorate their Christmas trees. Raymond, the eldest, and his wife Emily and their children would have small opaque glass balls, medieval elves, and strings of dried cranberries. Maybe even strings of popcorn. I think they would have had Helen and Charlie over for cranberry whiskey cocktails and Irish stew, and the whole family would string dried cranberries to drape on the tree.

Her daughter Angela was harder to guess. I think she was short of money. One day, when I was over, Helen was writing out a cheque for five thousand bucks. Five thousand big ones!

And though she asked me to, I kind of forgot to mail it for her, until she began to fuss because Angela had called to say she hadn't received it. I think maybe Angela would have homemade ornaments. Things like starched, hand-crocheted snowflakes and Styrofoam angels—a big one for the tree top—and knitted miniature socks with hard candies inside.

The youngest, Ben, would have all those moose characters and cartoon athletes and colourful birds and festive nests. I think he'd even put a bird on top of his tree. I'm not sure Helen would like that.

Raymond and his family took up a lot of space in Helen's albums. She would say, "They are very good to us," with a tone of voice that had a hint of indignation, as though there were those who were not so very good.

Angela lived in Nanaimo. "So," sniffed Helen, "we don't see her very often." I had the impression that Angela lived in Nanaimo just to aggravate her mother. Angela was divorced and her children had scattered across the mainland. This family seemed to be photographed in two batches each year, not including the school pictures they sent dutifully until the children graduated. One batch would have the thick Vancouver Island vegetation as a backdrop, taken at Easter when Helen and Charlie made their annual visit to Nanaimo. The other would be here in Helen's rock garden or around her cottage at Sylvan Lake, taken when Angela came out on vacation. Helen said *I* was like her second daughter and someday she would take *me* to the cottage.

Ben was hardly in any pictures after his childhood. His ex-wife and children were there more often than he was, and for the most part you would see him putting his hand up to block the camera's eye. Helen had more newspaper clippings of him than anything. Oh, I didn't tell you that she had a substantial set of scrapbooks as well.

Ben was in the news a lot. There's a story about him: when he was about twelve, he and two other boys from their hockey team went on strike to support their goalie, who had been suspended for uttering nasty words to the coach. The boys preferred to get rid of the coach, though they wouldn't say why. "We have good reasons," they were quoted as saying.

"What were they?" I asked. "What were the reasons?"

Helen just shrugged her shoulders.

"And who won out?"

"I don't remember," she replied in a vague sort of way.

In his thirties, Ben was featured in the *Calgary Herald*. He had started up Ben's Sport Shop on a shoestring and later parlayed it into a lucrative string of stores across Western Canada. There were photos of him presenting prizes to local athletes and accounts of him starting up the Handicap Games. He wore T-shirts or soccer shirts, probably from his store, and Helen would always click her tongue and shake her head with a mix of pride and disapproval. "You should dress up for the occasion. Especially when you're in a position like that!"

I made a point of dressing up when I went to her place, and she always commented on how nice I looked. I am in her photo albums too. Especially for the times I brought flowers or I wore a fancy dress. Then it was like a special occasion.

You'd think Ben would have made more of an effort for his mother, but it was Raymond that she seemed most fond of. She always told me how he used to help her with dinner or escort her to church or take her on trips with his family when her first husband died. I did sometimes wonder, though, what Raymond was up to. Like, what was in it for him? What made him such a peach?

Maybe he was just interested in the treasures she collected over the years. There was a miniature porcelain figurine, made in France, displayed in her china cabinet, a woman of the fifteenth century, with pouffed up white hair and delicate porcelain lace over a pink and burgundy gown. I think I would have liked being a lady in those times. Every time I visited I told Helen how much I loved that ornament. She said it was very dear, but maybe she'd have to will it to me since I liked it so much, and since I was so good to her. But, I thought, I wouldn't be surprised if Raymond and Emily nab it when Helen isn't thinking straight. And what if she dies suddenly? No one will know her intentions. And who knows if her family would honour them anyway?

Around November I thought to myself, I am going to have the most fabulous Christmas tree and I am going to invite Helen and Charlie over for Christmas cake and eggnog—like family. But I couldn't decide what kind of decorations to buy. I saw some crystal angels, but they were sooo expensive. Then Charlie passed away. Right before Christmas.

Helen was a widow again, so I began to go there twice a week to do errands for her, picking up groceries and medicine and mailing out letters. I was very good to her, but she got upset with me when her EpiPen disappeared and I forgot to pick up a refill at the drug store. I told her I was sorry. But she was annoyed. She said she would just have to search through her stuff, it was time she did that anyway, time she sorted things out and unloaded some of it before she was gone—if you catch her drift.

The very next day I decided to make her a Valentine's cake with her favourite seven-minute frosting, tinted pink of course, just to cheer her up. It was a maple chiffon cake with five egg yolks and eight egg whites. Eight! I didn't have enough vegetable oil so I topped it up with just a smidgen of peanut oil. Hardly any.

I wore my red silk blouse and black velveteen pants. She was thrilled and she wanted to take a picture of me holding the cake, but this time I insisted on taking one of her. She was going to hold the knife, like wedding couples do, and pretend to cut, but I think pictures should capture people in action. I insisted that she go ahead and just enjoy herself. I wanted to capture the true spirit of the occasion.

That was her last set of photographs. I took the film and

had it developed myself—it was time I started my own album.

No one in her family even asked who made the cake. I'm sure they could figure it out. After all I was the one who finally took her to emergency. I was the one who was there when she needed someone.

You have to know that I didn't even think about the peanut oil. I knew about the peanuts, but oil never crossed my mind. Honest to God!

I have that figurine on my dresser. I pick it up each night and polish it with one of Helen's silk hankies. I intend to take proper care of it. She meant for me to have it! And I do follow things she said, way more than her family ever would. I always make sure my hair and makeup are done just right, and I do dress for the occasion.

JANET STORIES

Life in Cars

❦

A MOTOR IDLES BELOW HER third-floor apartment. Janet peers downward through slanting blinds as interlude to her Audrey Hepburn movie marathon. She has seen these two before. Scruffy girls. Agitated blonde and tenacious brunette. This characterization is determined by the movement of their hands in the bucket front seats of the Jeep parked just below. The back seat is not visible. Brunette, with a round face and a medium bob, is the driver in more ways than one. She repeatedly calls or texts someone, then pulls out a packet from her bag, grabs a thick book from the back, and hands it to Blonde, who has been tossing and fingering her hair in a continuous replay of a shampoo commercial, except her hair is stringy. White powder is emptied on top of the book and lined up quickly. Janet has seen enough on TV to fill in details that she does not actually see here. Blonde bends over with what might be a straw and comes up even more unhinged. She looks out her side window, fixed yet twitchy and detached. Brunette inhales next. For her it seems like a chore, a job to be done. She packs her wares quickly like an Avon lady and wheels back out of the parking stall and down the lane. Two young girls. Someone's granddaughters.

Janet remembers life in cars when she was in high school, travelling with older boys in roomy sedans and classmate girls who aimed to prove they could easily smoke Number 7s and drink bottles of Pilsner or lemon gin, like the guys they hoped to impress. Girls apparently going wild as they vomited in ditches or made out with inebriated abandon, missing curfews, yet able to rebound for another week of school and another weekend in cars.

Blonde and Brunette parked here on a warmer day, two weekends before. Their rap music blasted up, heavy on the bass, through Janet's balcony doors, getting her attention in the first place. The girls twisted in their seats, dancing and flirting with evident bodies in the back. Blonde lowered her window, letting in cool air, and turned on her knees. She lifted her midi-T, flashing what Janet assumed were small bare breasts to those in the back. On drugs, she had thought at the time, and today it is confirmed.

Necking in cars was a staple in Janet's day. Maybe a hand made it under her sweater, even onto the cups of her bra, but it was mandatory to push the hand away, at least for a time. Copping a feel was supposed to be a happy accident. Discretion was understood, at least in the minds of girls. Even those who went on to become pregnant could be covered, in a magic show kind of way, with a wedding and tales of love and romance.

She has been watching *Roman Holiday* on cable. Love happens to Audrey Hepburn and reporter Gregory Peck. Audrey is a princess, under the spell of a sedative, kind of like Sleeping Beauty. Gregory discovers her asleep on a bench. She has escaped her country's embassy and her royal duties in the back of a delivery truck. He has no idea that she is the princess he is scheduled to interview. He awakens her, like a handsome prince, but she remains groggy and vulnerable, so he takes her to his apartment and makes sure she sleeps on his couch. (Understood—it is a movie from the fifties.) Even when the truth is known, once Audrey is back to travelling in limos, Gregory refrains from reporting her lapse in princesshood, and they acknowledge their love from afar.

Movie over, Janet peers through the blinds again while Macklemore plays. It's "White Walls," they say, on a preview to Video Countdown before the next movie starts, and she thinks about Blonde and Brunette. She usually flips the channel or makes some tea, but now she strains to hear the lyrics. He is singing about wanting to be free, to just live. Sounds a little sixty-ish to her, except he wants to do it all inside his Cadillac. And then Schoolboy Q chimes in about white hoes snorting coke in the backseat and inhaling his love. Well, Blonde and Brunette did remain up front.

    City police are parked in front of the building. The sky has turned grey and sundown is imminent. There is a skiff of snow on the ground. Janet wonders if the cruiser has a connection to the girls. It could save them in the long run, stop them in their shady tracks. She has wondered what she should do. Leave them to fate and avoid reprisals or report their business to the police? Identify herself as a busy body in case the police have been called here to deal with some other complaint? She checks through the blinds often, like a regular snoop, until she spots Blonde and Brunette coming from the Jeep in visitor parking across the lane. They are younger and scruffier than Janet expected now that she sees them whole. It is cold outside but Blonde just wears a top with off-the-shoulder straps. She is always cooling down. Brunette at least has her arms covered. They are like skittish mule deer as they eye the police car and then look up at her window. She quickly steps back as they slip into the building, then she listens for the elevator bell registering a stop on her floor and for footsteps along the hall. She does not know whether the girls live here or are frequent visitors. If they are visitors someone must buzz them in. She hears nothing.

    Two For The Road with Audrey Hepburn and Albert Finney. Janet hasn't seen it in forty years. It brings on nostalgia for the sophisticated death and resurrection of love and marriage, the transition from being an unencumbered single to a preoccupied parent and spouse. They travel through the south of France, in itself fuel to youthful yearning for adventure and romance, first backpacking, then in a series of cars. You can figure out their age and status in life by the car they are driving. A Mercedes-Benz, an MG, a Triumph, a Volkswagen bus, and a Ford station wagon are driven but not shown in chronological order, all to the music of Henry Mancini with someone singing about feeling fancy free.

Janet wasn't married when she watched the first time, but she had shed her teenage vision of marriage before sex. And Jack, her on-again-off-again boyfriend, who had gone to the movie with her, seemed elated to find in Audrey and Albert similarities in their own turbulent relationship. Even hope. They had walked, hitchhiked, bused, and eventually travelled in a second-hand Caprice, sometimes stopping along the highway between Edmonton and Calgary to satisfy horny desires. And they sang "Drive My Car" from The Beatles' *Rubber Soul*.

Elation was temporary and, like Audrey and Albert, she and Jack skirted fidelity. As they grew their hair long, they favoured freedom from commitment. Finally they married others when they didn't know what else to do.

Janet drives a new Ford Fiesta. It symbolizes a new beginning. She wanted red but settled for the less conspicuous ingot silver with a titanium interior. She rarely has passengers, except when her granddaughters stay, and they still always ride in the back. Twelve- and thirteen-year-olds who like their smart phones and their earbuds with their music kept private. They are the age her daughter was when she and Rich split. She adores them. Rich adores them too. Janet and Rich are retired, he from Cooperative Finances, she from The Gallery. Their two-storey house, a sanctuary for their daughter in the early years, holds a new generation family now. They have tried to cram history with divided belongings into their respective two-bedroom apartments. They have gone full circle back to the living arrangements they had when they first met, but the contents no longer know boundaries.

Henry Mancini's eerie and oppressive track, "Wait Until Dark," plays in minor-mode. No lyrics. The movie is a thriller. Audrey Hepburn is on the verge of divorce from Efram Zimbalist Jr. She is also newly blind from an accident, perhaps a metaphor for lapses of judgement in her life. At Kennedy Airport Efram, who travels regularly as a photographer, encounters a fashion model who asks him to hold a doll for her. Then she disappears. He takes the doll to his apartment, unaware that it is stuffed with heroin, and then he is tricked by the hoodlums, who have dibs on the dope, into going away again, leaving Audrey alone. There are many twists and turns, half of which Janet has forgotten. She is anxious and breathless and grateful for a commercial break to ease the tightness in her chest and the clamping of her fists, all in spite of the fact that she has seen this movie before, albeit forty years ago.

A dog is yapping down the hall. Janet looks through her door's peephole but sees no movement either way. That dog is lonely for sure. It too listens for the elevator bell. It is left in that apartment while its owner takes off in his SUV. His Nissan, always sparkling white, seems to be his baby, though the pavement underneath his tires is loaded with dirt and gravel. This she knows because their stalls share underground space between two posts and he tends to hog the space. It can be a tight squeeze to align the Fiesta, which she admits is often dusty or mud-spattered, into her spot.

Wait Until Dark is back on. Men come and go, impersonating police or friends of Audrey's husband in order to extract the doll from her. Janet realizes that Audrey does not seem to lock her door. She braces for the movie's climax. Heroin trafficker and psychotic killer Alan Arkin faces off with Audrey Hepburn, who smashes all the light bulbs in the apartment to put them on an even keel. However a stream of light is emitted when he opens the fridge door and violence ensues. Oh lord, Audrey stabs him with a kitchen knife and hides behind the refrigerator and pulls the plug. Janet hides her own face behind her afghan even though she knows what happens next.

There is a knock on Janet's door. She sits petrified in her chair and clicks mute on her TV controls in the hope that no one hears a sound from her apartment. The knock persists. No one ever comes to her door from within the building. Well, there was one time when a resident came to take the census before the provincial election. The woman was all business, not even commenting on the weather.

The sun has set. Janet sits in the dark with only an exterior light filtering in through the narrow openings of the blinds. The back of her dining room chair is levered just under the doorknob. Earlier she looked across the street to see the girls' jeep still in visitor parking. The police car is no longer in sight, but perhaps they are all being watched surreptitiously.

She puts on a bathroom light, due to the necessities of being human, in the windowless backside of the apartment. She is not blind so when she turns the light off again and goes back out she realizes the muted TV is casting shadows across the living room wall. The hallway is quiet and its lights still beam under her entry door. She decides to look through her peephole even though she knows it is inadequate, providing a limited range of view. Paper is at her feet. Someone has slipped it under the door. She turns her lights back on.

6:45 p.m. Parking stall # 24. Accidental dent and scratch in the side of your Ford Fiesta Licence # LTU 501. Contact my Insurance at 403-555-2211. Realize you were parked over the line. T. Holden Apt 312.

Janet hates dealing with issues. Should she go through the rigmarole? Tomorrow, when the world is awake, when the day is new, when light comes from the sun, when she feels safe, she will get dressed and go down and inspect the damage.

She always remembers that Gap commercial. *It's back, the skinny black pant.* The ad that uses AC/DC's song, "Back in Black." Audrey Hepburn dances in her black flats and her black turtleneck and black cigarette pants, back from the dead thanks to digital technology and to her dance routine from the movie *Funny Face*. Audrey says she just likes expressing herself and that she dances for release. Janet can certainly relate to that.

Police and Matisse

✻

HE DIDN'T SOUND LIKE A COP. Janet's phone rang and displayed the name of her apartment building. Someone was buzzing her line to let them into the building. It was hard to hear all that he said, but she did hear "Police Sergeant somebody or other" and "I need to get into the building."

"Pardon me? Did you say police?"

"Yes."

"But I don't know that you are."

"Okay." He didn't push.

She is pleased with the way she handled that call, then wonders if he will get in by buzzing someone else. Maybe he has a domestic restraining order and he is intent on revenge and murder. An apartment building holds so many possibilities and security is up to its residents.

She continues with her coffee and cheddar cheese and toast spread with crab apple jelly, catching a bit of the morning show on TV. Then it hits her that he might be legitimate and she might see a police car out front. She looks out across her balcony to the deserted road and to the identical apartment building across the way, then angles her view sharply to the left, leaning her cheek against the venetian blinds, and sure enough there is a city police car. It seems she has obstructed an investigation.

On the other hand she has heard of officers who are involved in their own domestic disputes. She has been following the case of that Winnipeg Mountie, Dietrich, who made jealous email threats toward his fellow officer, Donaldson, who is now married to Dietrich's ex-girlfriend. Donaldson transferred to Alberta out of fear for his life. Dietrich had threatened to "shoot and kill" and was now suspended from duty with pay and awaiting trial. These can easily be comments made in temporary madness.

She knows this. Her own ex-husband said similar things when he discovered her so-called "affair" with her director at The Gallery. Richard talked about getting a gun, which was a ridiculous notion. He had never had one in his hand. It was his own reputation he was worried about, and he used the very outdated "cuckhold" as reference to himself. His fellow accountants were a conservative lot, so it was all understandable that he would be concerned about their opinion. Artistic people tend to be more open minded, less judgemental, she likes to think.

Janet has tried to learn the details of Dietrich's trial, which was put off for three months because Donaldson's responses to the threatening emails were deleted. They were deemed critical to the defence and needed to be recovered. It is hard to find any further information in the news, even in online gossip. It is easy for her to see what else Dietrich could be. Investigating antisocial behaviour over several years with a gun in tow could surely bend the mindset of certain individuals. Perhaps if he had become a plumber or an electrician instead his view of relationships would revolve around a domestic life that expected order and function and safety in the pipes and wires and connections that held a household together.

The fact remains that, whether Dietrich is convicted or not, whether or not his intentions were to follow through with murder, he did send the emails. And the fact remains that Janet's "affair" was discovered when Richard snooped through her emails, both sent and received, whether or not her intentions were to follow through beyond the flirting messages.

Janet does not consider herself a flirt. She doesn't bat her eyelashes or use innuendos. She did however elevate Marc Chagall over her favoured Henri Matisse just to indulge her director's preference. He argued that Chagall's use of colour and dreamy content was the true representation of human connection, including humour and fantasy and love.

She was especially drawn to Chagall's lovers, who floated and embraced and caressed and even swooped for joy. She fantasized about herself in such scenarios with her director. She tried, however, to ignore Chagall's circus characterizations. For her, clowns and acrobats are symbols of folly, even psychological damage, but she still secretly follows stories like the criminal case of RCMP Officers Dietrich and Donaldson because of the mental distortion involved. Why do people resort to such drastic measures when simpler solutions are obvious? Why does anyone obsess about an ex-lover who obviously has moved on?

Richard was right that she was in her director's thrall but not right to confront him in the studio. How embarrassing for all. Though her retirement from The Gallery put an end to speculation, there was no going back to the marriage. And there is no longer reason to wax on Chagall. She has heard that her director is involved with the performance artist Sabine, who is known for taking *her* inspiration from Matisse's naked nymphs in *Joy of Life* and *La Danse*.

Janet second-guesses herself for the rest of the week. Police Sergeant so and so is probably legitimate, and he plays on her mind, though she has no idea what he looks like. She watches for a cruiser at all times of the day and night. She considers letting him in the building if he tries her again, though she knows she has probably warned him off of her number. Still it might bring her into the facts of his case. Guilty or innocent? That is always the question but never the whole story. If he does try her apartment again she could ask him to step out in front of the building so she can see him before she buzzes him in.

Snow comes down in stellar flakes, blowing toward the west and in sudden swirls. Ice coats the windshields of cars parked outside and crusts onto wipers. It is officially spring yet Janet can hear the scraping of a windshield. She looks down and across the blanketed road to see fresh paw prints followed by boot prints. Small dogs suitable for small spaces are routinely taken out to do their business before their owners leave for school or work. The loneliest dog, the one on her floor that barks nonstop when it is left alone, suddenly squeals, then stops its noise altogether. The eerie silence confuses the start of her morning. Should she call the police due to lack of noise?

Instead she reads the *Herald* with her coffee. There are no reports on Dietrich and Donaldson. She looks for information on The Gallery's itinerary or even her director's picture in the social pages, and she never misses the obituaries. She looks for him there just in case accident or illness has befallen him.

It seems like a good day to stay inside, to redo her apartment. Janet has gathered fabrics and cushions and throws and rugs in what she considers the style of Matisse. She read that he was born in a weaver's cottage and later collected fabrics throughout his travels, including his visits to Algiers and Morocco and Tangiers, and that his paintings depict exotic scenes because of the bright coloured stripes and diamonds and florals. Even his models are draped in patterns or sheers; the aura is harem-like.

Snow eclipses external sights and sounds. Janet, in a kind of fever, pulls out her mother's old Singer, determined to remember sewing skills learned years ago in Home Ec. She has settled on plum, azure, and tangerine for her colours, patterns à la Provence, with a mischievous touch of tartan, a bit of damask, and tapestry along with solid cottons and faux-silks. She forgets to have lunch, and when she finally looks out on her balcony, she sees a drift of snow hugging the planters. If this is today's version of spring, she'll block it out with her floral drapes. She unplugs the sewing machine and sets it back in its case, gathers scraps of cloth for the garbage, packs some of the old cushions and rugs for the thrift shop, and realizes she is starved. But first she changes into her new silk robe and pours a glass of Beaujolais to honour the occasion. Matisse would be comfortable here for sure. She opens a small round of boursin, breaks off chunks of baguette, cuts spears of pear, and sits in the most upright chair. Her silk robe gapes in the front as she poses her bare legs together at an angle.

The building is unusually quiet. She has not paid attention all day. The lonely dog, just three doors down, has not uttered a sound. She pours another glass of wine and contemplates explanations. Was it on some kind of vacation? Did those who complained about the barking and threatened to call SPCA succeed in having it taken away? She would miss that dog even if it sometimes annoys her too. It is, in a way, her warning system for activities in the hallway. Maybe its owner was home this day, never leaving its side. She can see that life could be lonely if you are always left behind. She looks around at her new boudoir and tries to imagine who would sit amongst the cushions, who would share a glass of wine, who would enjoy the silk of her gaping robe, who would happily pass the time. She pours wine again.

A knock on her door cuts through reverie, in fact startles her enough to spill wine on her robe and down one leg. She hesitates. It is repeated. She goes over and checks through the peephole. A cop stands dead ahead. At least he looks like one. This time she opens up.

"Hello, I'm Sergeant Hall." He pulls out his badge.

Janet has no idea what to check for. "Yes?"

"Did you notice anything unusual in the hallway today?"

"No, I've been really busy. Redecorating." She sweeps her right arm to the area behind her, as explanation, while her robe slides down her shoulder. "Why? Has something gone wrong?"

"There were complaints about a dog. Are you aware of any threats?"

"Well, yes, someone posted a note of complaint outside the elevator, but I have no idea who it was. Has something happened? To the dog?"

"Unfortunately, yes. Here's my card. If you think of anything, let me know."

"Sure." She pulls her robe a little tighter after she locks her door. She watches through her peephole and listens to the knocking on neighbours' doors along the hall. There is fear and excitement on her side of the door. It calls for another glass of Beaujolais and is followed by a slip into oblivion after such a busy day.

Her head aches in the morning while her stomach calls for food. She tends to both with aspirin and eggs, and then tries to read the *Herald*. She looks for news about her apartment building but guesses it is too new. But there is something else, finally. An update on Dietrich and Donaldson. It is about their latest day in court. Dietrich claimed he was just venting and never meant physical harm. He had no intention of killing Donaldson. She checks the obits in case her director is there, and then thinks about that poor lonely dog. What terrible harm has been done? It usually starts barking around this time when its owner leaves for work. Everything is quiet. Her new décor is impressive, but she can't seem to decide where to sit. She has to know what happened to the dog. She showers and dresses and makes ready to interrupt the janitor when he does his daily vacuuming along the hall.

"Hi," she says, her voice raised, as she opens her door. "Do you know what happened yesterday to the dog?"

He turns off the vacuum and cocks his Filipino ear.

"You know, the police came about the dog?"

He looks around then gestures with his hand down low as if pushing something with his fingers along the floor, toward a door. "Poison," he says and shakes his head.

"Oh no!"

He nods and shrugs, then turns the vacuum back on. She is left to close her own door. She hears on the morning news that tonight is the eve of a lunar eclipse, the night of a full blood moon. Some consider it an omen. She thinks about other tenants in a new suspicious light. You just never know who would resort to such a criminal act, but it must be someone right on her floor.

Janet assumes that people are not a target here, but she is uneasy as she walks down the hallway and rides the elevator down to parking. No one else is in sight. She has decided to go, one last time, to The Gallery to see if she has been missed at all.

There is a poster in the window. *Lunatic Artists*. She might have known her director would be ahead of the game, ready for the lunar eclipse. A carmine ball looms over mineral rock samples and sculptures, and a slide show clicks along on a back screen with the black-and-white footage of Apollo 11. Neil Armstrong and Buzz Aldrin are walking on the moon. Aside from all that, *lunatic* seems the predominate theme of paintings and collages and screen prints and photography: lunatic eyes, lunatic flowers, lunatic pin balls, even lunatic asylums. There is a wall of Pink Floyd's *The Dark Side of the Moon* sleeves repeated behind the cash desk.

"There you are. It's been a while," her director says as if he was expecting her to appear all along.

She sees that his hair, with streaks of grey, is longer and brushed straight back, and that he has let his beard grow out. He looks like Picasso's version of the satyr Silenus. She supposes that Sabine has influenced him.

"I see you are still alive," she says. "So, lunatics?"

"Hah, of course. And what are you up to?"

"Busy, very busy. Redecorating my place. Matisse is the inspiration."

"Ah."

"I was wondering if you had any self-portraits of him in your collection of prints." She had thought this up on her drive downtown.

"Strangely I think we do have one here. It is one from his younger days."

It is Henri Matisse in 1900 from the top of his head to his knees, standing in front of an easel with his brown hair combed back and a mustache and beard neatly trimmed. He looks very approachable. Of course he would.

"Perfect. I'll take it."

"House price for you," he says. "Nice to see you again, my dear."

His dear? She has turned into one of those familiar faces to whom he offers a deal for old time's sake. For the whole drive home, she tries to decide where she will hang her Matisse now that she has paid for it. It was never in the plan. Adjustments will have to be made. She can move the batik that hangs over the sofa so that the print can hang alongside. Or maybe Matisse can reside over the buffet where she can enjoy him every morning for breakfast. She does not let herself think about her director at all and least of all Sabine.

Two police cars are in front of her building, both with flashing lights. Though her parking spot is underground, she slows to a crawl then decides to wait outside in visitor parking where she can watch any kind of action. It is a young couple that the cops bring out. The two who live four doors down on the opposite side. She had already labelled them yuppies, though she knows they are younger than that. She noticed their commitment to a healthy life with their fancy joggers, their trim physiques, and their organic groceries stuffed into cotton totes. She has recyclable bags too but forgets to take them with her. She guesses that the barking was bad for their health. Some people just can't let things go.

Now that she has some answers, Janet continues on underground to her parking stall, uses her building key, rides the elevator to her floor, uses her apartment key, sets her Matisse print against the wall (portrait side out), and locks her door. Tonight she will raise the venetians, spring weather or not. She will take the winter covers off the balcony chairs, and even if it is after midnight she will sit outside to catch the total eclipse of the moon. She will wear a jacket and blankets and boots if necessary. She will witness her first blood moon, a lunatic moon, an omen so they say. Omen for what she does not know. Maybe Dietrich can move on and find a new love and Donaldson and his wife can forgive him and live in peace. She knows, however, that she must be real. The court will decide how it really ends. She'll check the *Herald* tomorrow but try to skip the obituaries.

Hair Matters

THE DYLAN THOMAS POEM runs through Janet's brain like a song: "And death shall have no dominion." She stares at herself in the mirror as she sits in the maroon swivel chair with her feet on the chrome footrest, but she does not swivel. There are mirrors all around so she can view the room from several angles. Hard to say what goes through the minds of the others in their chairs.

Janet is here for her Friday appointment. She has never before been tied to a certain day of the week to have her hair done, let alone a Friday, but she found out that this is Shirley's day off and she has switched to the much younger Megan who is the same age as her own daughter. Megan is taller than Shirley, so she pumps the chair a little higher in order to apply the golden dye to Janet's mostly white hair. Megan has a sunnier disposition than Shirley, is soon to be married, and keeps a more natural look with her own hair. It is long and blonde, and she sometimes just puts it in a ponytail, simple but still fashionable. This is more in keeping with Janet's style. At least her style when she was twenty. When she was young Janet also had long hair, left to tumble as hair will when left alone. To this day, when she hears David Crosby sing "Almost Cut My Hair," tears come to her eyes. It could be because of the pain in David's voice; she knows he is not just singing about plying scissors. Hadn't his girlfriend just died in an accident?

Janet was Shirley's client for about a year. She envies women who know they are the one to be served, not the other way around. Instead of openly choosing a stylist at any given time Janet became indebted to Shirley and now, like anyone avoiding their debtor, she sneaks in on Shirley's day off so she will not have to explain her shift in loyalty, as if she is a traitor.

Just last week, out of the blue, curious thoughts crossed Janet's mind. Was Shirley still working at the salon? Did she have enough clients to pay the bills? As it turns out some kind of intuition was at work in Janet's mind. Unlike a lot of these relationships Shirley unloaded to Janet about her difficult life. Usually it is the hairdresser who hears all the gossip. It got to be a little too much, worrying about Shirley, a woman the same age as herself. A woman who was divorced and had to sell her house and move to an apartment, not unlike herself. One big difference was that Shirley's hair did not have a hint of movement. It was clipped close to the head, shaved thin at the neck, streaked blonde and sprayed so that not a hair was out of place. Meticulous and not what Janet wanted for herself. Shirley was wound into a tidy skein except for the yellowed fingers and nicotine breath. Janet could not imagine Shirley in her twenties with braided daisies in her hair, disdaining corporations and Americans in Vietnam, listening to Bob Dylan sing "Lay Lady Lay," inhaling marijuana and in fact wanting to get laid, as the expression still goes. What would they have in common?

In her last gasp of single life, travelling abroad, Janet went to the musical *Hair*. Nudity was new on stage agendas at the time so it was a kind of titillation. But more to the point was how the protest of the Vietnam War and established ways of thinking manifested in the uninhibited growth of people's hair. It had nothing to do with a trip to the hair salon And then there was "Easy To Be Hard." She still plays Three Dog Night's version of it, and it runs through her mind inexplicably on this day, how people can be so heartless. Love was not always in the air for the one right in front of you. It was easier to emote for a cause.

Janet leans closer to the mirror. Her hair is coated with creamy dye, and sections stick out in all directions. Some of her scalp is painted too, especially around the edges of her face. It makes her skin look pasty white, even a little grey. Her wrinkles are not as prominent, but then she acknowledges that without her glasses they do seem to fade away.

Megan always gives Janet a copy of the latest celebrity gossip magazine to while away the time while her hair oxidizes. Janet learns who is a binge eater, who is pregnant, who miraculously has her trim body back after the birth of baby number one, who is planning a spectacular wedding for the third time, who lives with plastic surgery nightmares, and who, out of two, best wore a duplicate outfit. It is all irrelevant to her life so a relief for that very reason. At home she reads the obituaries to see who is still alive.

To be fair Shirley did ask questions about Janet's personal life and at first Janet let secrets roll off her tongue. But she began to ask herself why she would confide in someone she barely knew and didn't even relate to; it felt like going to a priest for confession when she is not Catholic or to a psychiatrist for diagnosis when she already knows her own foibles, except priests and psychiatrists are sworn to secrecy. Megan's life seemed easy and optimistic, with a wedding in the works and a home in the suburbs to settle into. Shirley, on the other hand, was meeting men online and had even moved in with one of them for a time followed by her own cynical analysis. Megan was too young to be curious about the romantic or sexual lives of women their age, as if Janet and Shirley were too old for such passions. Now, with Megan, the conversations remain uncomplicated and limited to the achievements of Janet's granddaughters, the changing of the seasons, the births and deaths of certain friends and relatives, and the style of Megan's wedding dress. She must ask Megan how she will do her hair with the veil.

Janet thinks it is odd that people will share intimate stories with those they barely know. It reminds her of her previous next-door neighbour, Monica, who liked to joke about her stint at Al-Anon where they operated on a first-name-only basis. Monica became "best friends" with one of the women in the group as they divvied out similar stories each week about surviving the tribulations of their drunken husbands. The friend ended up in hospital, and when Monica went to visit she realized she did not know her best friend's last name so she was not able to see her. Monica shared this story so many times, first with tears and then with laughter, that Janet almost felt she had joined Al-Anon herself. She thinks about this now because she realizes she does not know either Megan's or Shirley's last name. And if she had known Shirley's last name she would not have missed her in the obituaries.

It was lung cancer. And the chemo was short-lived since the cancer spread so rapidly. Would it be rude to ask if Shirley lost her hair? Is it insensitive to think about the irony of it all? A line from *Hair*, about keeping hair shoulder length or longer, runs through Janet's mind again as Megan snips away. She acknowledges that she can now make an appointment on any day of the week.

Janet never lost her hair, but it is short. Perhaps it is foolish to think this deemphasizes her wrinkles. Turns out she did have something in common with Shirley. More to the point she still comes to the salon once every month on the days that Megan is available. Any day of the week will do, unless of course she decides to make a change. It is odd how one becomes indebted over hair.

"You know, when I was your age I cheated on my husband," says Janet.

"Oh!" says Megan.

"Before we had our daughter, you know. So how will you do your hair for the wedding?"

Jumping to Conclusions

❀

SHE KNOWS IT IS CHILDISH but cannot stop herself. Janet drove into her underground parking stall on Tuesday and saw the black garbage bag right at the end of her stall. Jumping to conclusions is her pet peeve about others, but she assumed that the bag had been placed there by the occupant of the right-hand stall since it sat closer to that side. She turned off her engine, grabbed her purse and her bottle of merlot, locked her Fiesta with her remote key, and then grabbed the bag and plunked it right down at the end of her neighbour's stall. How dare someone dump their garbage on her! And now here it is back in front of her. She moves quickly this time. She puts the bag back in the right-hand stall and heads to the elevator before anyone sees her.

Inside her apartment, she takes off her boots, hangs up her jacket, and goes straight to the window. The window is where she goes to calm her nerves. She looks out across her balcony to the grove across the road, a small stretch of nature to the right of apartment buildings and between her and the strip mall. She spied mule deer foraging there in December. There is a hint of green on the tips of the trees. Maybe spring is coming after all. She ignores the apartments across from her. They extend more to the west. Windows are covered, curtains drawn, venetians closed; strangers are all trying to keep safe and secure, shutting out neighbourly probes.

She is cutting a chicken into parts and dropping skin and

bones into her kitchen garbage when she suddenly wonders what might be in that black bag. She hadn't bothered to check. She questions the state of her mind. When she cleaned out her car, after her granddaughters stayed, she put their wrappers and apple cores, along with cardboard from the trunk, into a black garbage bag. Has she forgotten that she set the bag temporarily against the wall? Is the garbage really hers? Is she losing a grip on her mind? No. She remembers taking it to the bins. It isn't a difficult chore. So why would anyone leave their garbage to her? They are insulting her for sure.

If it happens again, if it is put back in her stall, she should open the bag just to see what is inside and look for clues about the owner. But as she imagines herself doing just that, she recoils and envisions herself with contaminated hands, with what she does not know.

Sure enough the bag is back the very next day, and this time there is a ripped piece of paper under her windshield wiper. Janet is heading to the South Health Lab, but gets back out of the car to retrieve it and read it even though she is running late. It is printed in awkward letters as though it was done in a hurry. *This Is Not My Garbage! Do Not Put It In My Stall!* She goes over a response in her mind. "Jumping to conclusions! It's not mine either. Childish both ways you know." She searches her purse at least three times so she can reply right away on the back of that paper and put it on the window of that neighbour's van, but she can't find her pen. Perhaps it is just as well. "Take your time this time," she says to herself.

She is going to her appointment. She knows all about this routine, the callback, since she had surgery and radiation two years before. It is a different lab though. She has since moved from her house and neighbourhood of thirty years to an apartment further south. The complex is full of immigrants, including children and pets, who will move on to their Canadian dream homes as soon as they can, and young singles out of their parents' homes for the very first time, plus a few like herself who have abandoned the dream and settled into apartment ennui.

The Health building is only three stories high, but it takes up a block in length and has more than one entrance. Janet is oblivious to signs giving her directions. She is still fuming about the bag. She parks and then once on foot she reads the signs and clips along to the lab at the other end of the parking lot, knowing she is late. Cool morning air refreshes her brain until she finds herself in the waiting room after all. She renews her angst over the bag of garbage. She cannot help herself.

She is used to stripping down to her waist and leaning against the cold metal machine while the technician positions each breast in turn between the parallel plates. The plates come together and compress the tissue as flat as flat can be until the buzzing sound tells her she is zapped by a remote with ionizing radiation. Experience comes with age for sure, but not with reassurance. She'll treat this like any other day and deal with results on another day.

She heads straight back home and presses her own remote to enter the underground parking lot. Her neighbour's van is gone. She could open the garbage bag and look inside, but she is repelled and cannot stand to touch it. She will go up to her apartment and get a pen. Better yet she'll take the ripped paper upstairs and compose her response in a thoughtful way instead of her knee-jerk reaction.

Janet returns in the evening when she least expects direct confrontation. She places her polite reply—*My Apologies, But It's Not My Garbage Either*—under the windshield wiper of the van, then notices the bumper sticker for the very first time. *Thou Shalt Love Thy Neighbour As Thyself*. Okay, she has a religious person on her hands. This was not on the van before. Is this little message just for her? Who does bumper stickers? Not anyone she knows well.

It is the Festival of Crafts at Stampede Park on Mother's

Day weekend, which Janet is spending alone. She is going to see the latest work of artisans and artists. She might pick up some exotic tea or a bag made from reclaimed leather or funky jewellery for her granddaughters. She has stopped looking at jewellery for herself. But first she checks out the paintings. Though she's retired from The Gallery, she likes to imagine who she would pick for a showing. Next to a display of Rocky Mountain watercolours is a booth called Fun Laser Designs. This is not exactly art to her, and of all things they sell bumper stickers. She is not an impulse buyer, but this is pure serendipity. Starting on the left side of a sticker, *This Is Earth* is printed in blue letters. In the middle is the Earth orb with green continents and blue oceans, and on the right is *Not Uranus. Keep It Clean.* She whispers it to herself. "This is earth, not Uranus. Keep it clean."

It is hard to explain her joy and urgency to go home and clean off her bumper. Maybe she needs new avenues for self-expression. She presses the sticker to the right side of her bumper as it will be closer to the van and more likely to be seen. She is aware that the bag of garbage is still on her side but decides to leave it alone.

Upstairs she prepares frozen shrimp for her stir-fry and listens to "Black Magic Woman" by Santana. She lifts each shrimp out of the bowl of cold water, pulls off the legs, and peels back the shells. Heads snap off too. Then she holds the bodies and pulls off the tails. What would an x-ray of a shrimp look like? She cuts down the backs with her paring knife and pulls out digestive tracts with a toothpick. Sometimes she has trouble getting it all. Each time she drops refuse into the kitchen garbage she envisions the bag down in the parking lot. What would an x-ray of that bag reveal? She puts on Harry Nilsson's "I Can't Live" instead of Santana, pours a glass of pinot grigio, and sings along while she throws shrimp in proper turn with veggies into the sizzle.

On Sunday morning Janet goes to her car, though she does

not have a destination in mind. Nothing has changed in either stall. The bag still sits in hers. She might as well go on to the drive-through at Tims to get a French-vanilla coffee. She is drawn to bumper stickers on cars as never before. The Mazda in front says *Pay It Forward*, and the driver lives up to its slogan. Her coffee is paid for, says the girl at the window. "How nice," she mutters and lurches forth, then realizes she could have repeated the favour.

As days go by Janet has to remind herself to pay attention to traffic, as she is now compelled to look for and read every bumper sticker on the road. And each time she pulls into her stall she is reminded to do something about the bag. For one last time she sets it right on the dividing line. It could belong to either side.

She is not disappointed. The van responds. *What Would Buddha Do?* The background is a rainbow of colours, and a green Buddha sits on the left of the white letters. But wait. The last message came from the Bible. Where is the conviction?

Janet heads out to the location for Decals and Signs. She found directions on the internet while ignoring the mail that sits on her counter. It is mostly impersonal anyway except maybe the one from Diagnostics. The shop is in a light industrial area, and the woman behind the desk is mainly taking calls or working the computer. She looks up at Janet in surprise.

"I'm looking for bumper stickers," says Janet.

"What did you have in mind?"

"Well, that depends. I'll know it when I see it. I thought you would have some on display."

"We have a catalogue. You can have a look. What kind of business is it for?"

"Not exactly a business. A project, I guess you could say."

She sits in the one leather chair by the window and flips through the pages. There must be some logic, some kind of catalogue order, but Janet is unable to figure it out. And she can't bring herself to ask for assistance. She is about to give up when she reads the motto, *Never Give Up* with the line underneath, *Hope-Love-Care*, punctuated with a pink ribbon. Okay, she will continue a little longer. Perhaps this is a sign.

She writes three possibilities down, along with their order number. *If You Change Nothing, Nothing Will Change* is printed in bold black letters. *Don't Believe Everything You Think* is in purple italics, and the third sticker has *Caution* printed within a yellow triangle followed by *This Vehicle Is A Transformer*. That last one could be perceived only as a reference to a toy, and the neighbour may miss her meaning, so she strikes it out. She settles on getting just two.

"You've made a choice?"

"Yes."

"Good. How many would you like? They come in bundles of fifty but are cheaper by the hundred."

"Oh." She is embarrassed to back out. "I guess I'll just take the one in a bundle of fifty. Number six three oh five. Don't believe everything you think."

"Pardon me?"

"The sticker says don't believe everything you think."

"Oh," the woman laughs and Janet laughs too.

As soon as she reaches her apartment, she opens the package, gets two rags, one damp and one dry, and goes back down to buff her bumper clean, especially on the left side where she affixes her new sticker, *Don't Believe Everything You Think*, right next to *This Is Earth, Not Uranus. Keep It Clean*. It feels good to accomplish things each day. The black bag still sits on the border.

It is the next afternoon and the van is still parked. The bumper already has its stickers but above, right next to the licence plate, is a new sticker: *I'm With Nietzsche!* But how does that fit with a Christian commandment and an allusion to the teachings of Buddha? Is this an accusation of false ethics? She knows she has been childish and maybe a little crazy but never with mean intent. She moves to open the bag after all, in case it holds some wicked truth, and then she will take it to the bins. How could she know that once her mind was made up the option would be gone? How could she know that the bag would be gone?

This Easter Janet is cooking a stuffed turkey for her daughter and granddaughters and some old neighbourhood friends. She will extend her table for the first time since her move to this apartment. It is a day that she hopes they will cherish. She has sorted her jewellery to give to the girls instead of what she might have bought at the Festival of Crafts. She won't explain her affair with bumper stickers.

It is late morning. She pulls out the heart and the liver and kidneys as well as the frozen neck and drops them into the kitchen garbage. This is typical North American waste, but she has no patience for cooking parts that were repackaged in an otherwise empty cavity. Her hands are cold and have a touch of raw turkey juice on them. She washes them under the tap with dish detergent. The letter from Diagnostics is still unopened on the ledge above the sink, and she has yet to return her doctor's call. She is listening to Procol Harum. She never remembers all the lyrics but joins in on a certain repeated line about a ghostly face turning pale.

She suddenly remembers that she has left a package of sage on the passenger seat of her car, so she takes the elevator down to the parking lot. Her neighbour with the van is gone for good. Strange that they never met. A couple with a Kia Soul hatchback, fixed with a toddler car seat in the back, parks there now. It has one small bumper sticker. *Albania.* She guesses they are starting a new life in a new country but are missing their old home. Now what can she do with that?

SORRY HEARTS

Fee Fine

❀

LEONA MCADAMS SITS AT HER small wooden table in her small wooden chair (to her limited knowledge no one else sits there, so the table and chair are hers) and plays with her cream of wheat. She uses her spoon to draw the milk into rivulets that expand and flood islands of sugar, then she mixes it all together. The table is situated close to the boy's crib. She hears him whimper and squirm, blankets rustling, and she can no longer contain her curiosity. She peeks through the bars at the boy with no name; she is anxious she might be committing an offence, but she observes him nonetheless.

The boy, who sometimes squalls, often sleeps, can only kick up his heels in his crib, whereas Leona, once let out of hers, can pick up and wander away. Suddenly he begins to scream. She has spied on him. She has broken a rule, real or imagined. She quickly runs back to her chair and shoves a glob of porridge into her mouth.

At the age of three Leona has been left to recover from an appendectomy at St. Mary's Hospital, founded by the Sisters of Providence, fifty-two miles from home. She might as well be across the world, for at this point she has no sense of distance and even if she did it wouldn't matter. The first (and last) time her parents tried to leave at the end of visiting hours she sobbed and clung to their necks, their collars, their coats, whatever she could reach and grab.

Leona's mother will someday explain the Sisters' advice: that it was better to stay away and avoid upsetting her at their leaving. Better to heal the cigar shaped scar running vertical on the right side of her belly button. Otherwise her fevered contortions to claim hold of her parents might tear the stitches apart.

Feeling abandoned, Leona determines that the two, her mother and her father, who up to this point she has counted on, can no longer be fully trusted. Or, she considers, though never fully conceptualizes, that the reverse could be true. Perhaps she *has* committed an offence and *she* cannot be trusted.

Leona's parents have instilled good behaviour when it comes to strangers, even those who seem to hide all but a well-scrubbed face and hands. Now that she is mobile the Sisters often sit her on a very tall stool (at three everything is tall) at their work station at the end of the hall. They provide pencil and paper and encourage her to draw. They hover and rave about her scribbles and pat her blonde curls; they adopt her knowing full well the temporary nature of these maternal episodes, and she basks in their praise. She will have no memory of speaking to these women whose ears are, in any case, covered with veils.

When her parents come around the corner, smiling and anxious to take her home, Leona pretends not to see them. She heads in the opposite direction, wearing her striped cotton dressing gown, straight to her work station and her new guardians.

Of course she returns to the white bungalow with the small veranda and the add-on back porch. It is the exterior that she savours, the yard protected by a caragana hedge at the front and the crabapple spreading across the back. She inhales sweet fragrance as she runs circles around the purple lilac, heeding warnings (inspiring temptation) to stay clear of the honeysuckle with its pink flowers in spring and carmine berries in summer. Clusters of tulips conjure the land of wooden shoes as it was depicted on the cover of her mother's *Better Homes and Gardens*, stoking an awareness of foreign places.

Leona is now five. Tiger lilies and peonies form backdrops for paper dolls; snap dragons are pinched into novelty jaws; pansies show faces with nursery-rhyme names; poppies, delicate and satiny, seem sturdy nonetheless and determined to pop up wherever they wish. Petunias, geraniums, gladiolas, and begonias are a parent's affectation, planted in precise order.

The interior of the house is another matter; it is full of minefields.

"Oh yes. You're the Big-I-Am," says her mother to her father. "I am sick. I am tired. I am hungover?"

"For God's sake," he pleads.

Leona has no idea what it is about, but instinct tells her to take a side. "Don't call him that," she says.

He takes another swig of cough syrup, pours another cup of tea, adds more milk and sugar (four teaspoons), lights another Craven A, has a spate of coughing, and shrinks a little more. He doesn't look big at all.

Leona pushes her oatmeal porridge with her spoon, compressing it into an island in the middle of the bowl. She adds more brown sugar to a depression in the centre, but it leaks into the moat, turning the milk amber.

Earlier she awoke to their subdued voices floating through her bedroom window, a blessed time when the two are up at daybreak to work in the garden and are careful not to disturb the town. She stayed cozy in her bed, feeling part of a contented household, unlike the times when she covers her head to shut out one of their fierce disputes.

Later in the day she will pull young carrots from the earth and spray dirt off with the hose and pick peas from the vines. She has perfected the snapping open of pods, counting (she can count to one hundred if asked) and plucking one pea at a time—all delicious.

But at breakfast she feels motherly; she wants her father to expand, not withdraw. She chooses a spoonful of porridge where brown sugar has accumulated and formed a dollop of sweetness, but then she follows this with a pale spot of oatmeal—no sugar at all.

"Stop playing with your porridge," says her mother. "And don't talk to me like that. You have far too much sugar there. Like your father. That tea is syrup. Why bother with the tea?"

"Leave her be," says her father.

"Oh yes. Take her side. Let her do whatever she wants. If you're so G-damn smart you can keep your nose out of your books for a while and watch what she does. You just spoil her."

"I hate you," says Leona, joining the defence. She will use these words as weapons for years to come, but for now she says it under her breath. Yes, she is more like her father. The lines are drawn.

Oatmeal does not slip as easily down a constricted throat. Leona is alone at the table, required to finish her breakfast. Her mother is in the bathroom, as she says, "putting on her face."

Her father has a business, McAdams Insurance, which covers house, automobile, crop, disability, and the big one, life. It is small, serving the locals. He runs it with his partner Uncle Gib who likes to quote David Hume and refer to utilitarianism when explaining his move from philosophy to insurance. They are compatible, the brothers—one self-educated through his library of books, the other prodded on by his professors. They discuss causation (aside from the damage of hail storms), inductive as opposed to deductive reasoning, realism, atheism, social relativism, and other isms. Customers enjoy these conversations and Leona, now eleven, loves to listen and put in her two cents; she knows good from bad, right from wrong.

She decides that her mother is community volunteer *ad nauseum* due to being president of this and that. She has learned the expression from Uncle Gib who studied at the University of

Alberta. He says it means "too much of anything." (She loves the *nauseum* part, though she usually talks about wanting to throw up.)

On this day Leona and her mother do a tour of both Crawfords and Wongs, the general stores in town. Mrs. McAdams requests a deal on flannel sheets and blankets and towels for the Milton boys, all to be paid for by The Women's Institute. The Miltons are not really boys. They are grown men with boys' minds, apparently inherited, through the generations, from the mother's side of the family.

Larry Milton is the sweet-natured one. The one that kids can tease without fear of retaliation. It goes like this:

"How you fee, Larry?"

"I fee fine." Larry grins, basking in the recognition.

"You fee fine, Larry?"

"Fee fine." Larry nods. Sometimes he is slurping, and occasionally dribbling his coffee, loaded with lots of cream and sugar, at the counter of the Royal Café, while his teenage interrogators call to him from a booth as they sip their cokes. Leona's friends, being younger, repeat this out on the street.

"How you fee, Larry?"

"Fee fine," he says and giggles and reaches out to shake hands with these smaller, less intimidating fry. Leona draws back but her friend Shelly puts her hand out, touches his sleeve, and then quickly pulls back and laughs at her trick. Larry laughs too. They all laugh until Larry drools; then, of course, they laugh even harder. That is until Sid—the oldest brother, the mean one—comes out and cuffs Larry. Though Larry tries to duck, he gets slapped on the ears and yelps then whimpers as he moves along. This reminds Leona of *The Three Stooges*, when Moe pokes Curly in the eyes. She doesn't think the Stooges are funny, but sometimes she laughs a kind of nervous choking laugh along with the crowd at the Saturday matinee.

The Milton brothers head toward the highway, out past the edge of town, with Sid in the lead and Larry close behind. A third brother must be waiting at home. They are bachelors, without mother or father.

Shelly, always braver than Leona with those on the fringe, hollers, "You don't have to be so mean, Sid," once the boys (really men with greying hair) are at least a block away.

Leona rides along to the ramshackle house, about a ten-minute drive from town. The bedding and towels are laid out in bags in the trunk. She stays in the Ford while her mother gets out; the brothers are already out in the yard, watching to see who has driven onto their property. Mrs. McAdams, even braver than Shelly, Leona thinks, talks to Sid while Larry grins and nods and Walter, the third brother, hovers on the porch. Sid follows her to the car and Larry follows Sid. After she loads the bags into their arms, Larry sticks his face up to the window and grins at Leona. Leona presses the lock.

"How you fee?" he asks and giggles until Sid kicks him in the shins and Larry yelps and they head toward the house.

Leona turns twenty just a week before Uncle Gib calls and tells her to come home. She takes the Dayliner then heads straight to the hospital, straight to the room, and stands at the foot of her father's bed. She has fretted over this inevitability since she can remember. The bars are halfway up on one side to prevent him from falling out—not very likely as he barely moves and what's left of his body disappears into the mattress. She moves to the open side and takes his hand. He presses hers just enough to confirm their lifelong pact, then relinquishes all effort, as though his life is in her hands. Her mother says he complained about being cold and accused her of turning down the thermostat, which she had not done in spite of what he says. And he was smoking again. He can't put that one over on her.

Leona wants to talk about abstracts, like love and admiration and even dying, though there is the issue of annihilation. She has lately been enthralled with existentialism, via Dostoevsky and, of course, Professor Coghill, who is her secret lover, but now she is stunned speechless and careful not to upstage her mother. She feels both rational and out of this world..She agrees to go back to the house for supper. As her mother insists, "We do need to eat." He dies alone while they are gone. It is hard to say who has abandoned who this time.

Leona's grandson Jamie calls "Grammie!" from the bedroom, at the end of his nap. He watches Leona through the crib bars, clutching his thin flannel blanket and beaming as she reaches for him. She kisses his cheek. He smiles, even raises his eyebrows, and kisses her back with his standard, wet, open-mouth smacker, right on her cheek. Unconditional love, both ways. Leona, née McAdams, now Fraser, soon to be McAdams again in spite of avoiding argument with *her* husband, has just turned sixty. For the first time, after all this time, for no reason she can think of, she is curious about the boy with no name who she spied on in the hospital all those years ago.

She has Jamie in her arms as she twirls and struts around the living room to James Brown. "I feel good," she sings along a little breathlessly, and plays the goof that a two-year-old appreciates.

"I got *you* Grammie."

"Yes, you have now," she sings

"I fee goot," he sings in his two-year-old way, and Leona, for the first time in many years, thinks about Larry Milton and her mother's charity, as well as the boy in the hospital with no name. The boy will be pushing sixty now if he has made it this far, and Larry Milton is probably dead like her father. Jamie's hairline is, so far, like those receding on middle-aged men, and his hair is still thin, like the boy with no name—the one thing she remembers about the boy.

Jamie's mother, Leona's daughter, Leanne, has a full head of hair now, beautiful strawberry blonde, but at fifteen, when the marriage was falling apart, her hair fell out—first the odd strand, then handfuls. Leona's son Jon, on the other hand, has always kept his hair growing wild and strong, perfumed with tobacco and pot. He plays his guitar and claims a mellow sensibility, but Leona suspects anger is burning at the core. He and his band mates have *discovered* James Brown and try to claim him as their own. For her the music is nostalgia or, at times, a reminder of the long-ago use of sex to manage mourning.

Leona twirls Jamie faster, harder. "I feel nice," she sings and she really does feel nice. She wonders if James Brown felt nice when he sang it. Was he free of self-reproach or, like her, did a sense of guilt often travel with him?

The Guardian

❋

SHE IS MY LITTLE GIRL. She sits with a pensive mouth and unequivocal eyes. "I'll have my breakfast now," she commands.

I am at her beck and call. I am dispensing a mother's cure.

I realize she has a beautifully shaped head. It has just a few gentle wisps of hair remaining, but, if she were given permission, she would be beautiful bald.

There is a picture of her, as a young girl, standing in front of the poplar in our yard, its slender green limbs reaching up with hopeful energy. She has long braids, her hair pulled close to her head, her head cocked wistfully downward, her eyes screening the light.

The poplar must have taken root innocently enough, producing miniature leaves that would jitterbug in the breeze. But in my earliest memory the poplar was already grown and reaching over to my bedroom window.

It had smooth, grey skin with comfortable black botches that I would trace and read with my fingers. Black ants would lead a procession to the patches of sticky sap, and I would summon them forth and urge them on in low funereal tones, like a director whispering orders over a loudspeaker.

I would sit in its shade and strip caragana pods, putting the moist, green seeds into miniature porcelain cups. I would offer her a sip if she happened by, and she would thank me and pretend to enjoy my concoction.

This morning I stir the oatmeal as if I am in a trance, vaguely aware of the bubbles erupting into miniature volcanoes. I stir and stir, stir and stir.

I lift her from the couch, placing my arm and shoulder under hers. I think, as always, that I will be too weak to support her, since she is my older sister, but I am strong, very strong. I am strong and powerful, and she is my little girl. I feel her ribs and the soft sides of what remains of her breasts.

"I'll have a little more milk, please. And could you put the sugar right in the middle? Thank you."

The porridge is good for her. She has more colour in her cheeks.

"I'll help you with your bath now," I say cheerfully. "Then we'll leave for the hospital."

I remember a time, in the dry summer heat, after shifting restlessly through the night, when my poplar branch began rubbing the window screen and dust began seeping in with the breeze. I looked out to find that the large heart-shaped leaves had developed a greyish appearance. They soon had a yellow mottling, and, as time passed, they turned a muddy brown and began to drop to the ground. People said that the tree was an eyesore. A band of Cygon was painted on the trunk, just below the lower branches, to kill off the gall-forming mites. I was told to stay away from my tree.

There had already been complaints about its greedy roots, how they sopped up so much moisture, leaving the grass roots high and dry and patchy. Sometimes the roots had surfaced above the ground, revealing the fact that they were creeping toward the foundation of our house. They had begun infiltrating our mother's prize flower beds and extending into the neighbour's yard. They showed no signs of self-restraint.

Chemotherapy room number four has chartreuse walls with pale magenta baseboards. At its centre is a green vinyl lounge chair, much like a dentist's chair without the usual paraphernalia. A woman with a long dark wig sits in reluctant repose and engages in an intense, animated conversation with her bearded companion. He leans over her, engrossed in her every word, as though they are sharing a cappuccino at some trendy coffee house. They seem oblivious to the intravenous tubing attached to her arm.

Across the hall, I see my girl laying obediently prostrate, looking small and solitary, with a catheter emptying down to a plastic bag of pink liquid. I stand outside her door and study the framed pallet of spring colours on the wall. Pure blues, pinks, peaches, and greens wash gently across the canvas. Two young girls in their long, blooming dresses and wide-brimmed hats—one a tall, willowy redhead, the other a cherubic, golden blonde—are looking wistfully downward and vaguely toward one another, but their eyes do not meet. In the background, a white picket fence progresses along in gentle rhythm, bordered by fresh green trees and bushes. On the frame is a gold plate inscribed: *In appreciation of the fine care given.*

In spite of the Cygon, the poplar's leaves continued to drop. I would wake up to a gentle scratching on my window and look out to see the skeletal finger of my naked tree pointing, accusingly, through the glass. Below, flagrantly coloured begonias bobbed for my attention. I would pull the covers over my head and listen to the birds announce, in muted tone, their pleasures and their fears, and I would believe that all was well and normal outside my window.

One morning a buzzing sound drew me out of bed and to the window, where I saw a slender, pale-faced man aiming a drill straight toward the heart of my tree. He began drilling a hole just a couple of inches toward the centre. He then withdrew and moved around the base of the trunk, drilling a ring of holes all around it.

I stood motionless, transfixed.

Setting the drill down, he lifted a can and poured liquid into each hole.

"I don't want any visitors today. Tell people I have plans."

"Okay," I say, smiling gently down as I pack the pillows in around her brittle, bony frame.

We sit in careful contemplation, then begin to share selected stories from our past. Our eyes meet momentarily, then stare into imaginary distances, holding tight to our deepest disappointments, our greatest fears, and our secret joys.

"I'll have some tea and chocolate cookies. Don't bring me vanilla. I'm in the mood for chocolate."

We engage in gentle smiles and gentle revelations. We gingerly sip our tea, careful not to burn our tongues.

We've been polite and gentle sisters. Good girls. Solemn good girls. Not likely to say, "I want this, I don't want that."

Now she makes it clear. "I've talked enough now. And no more phone calls."

I shift from dreams to semi-consciousness. Something is at my window. At first I think it is my tree, but then I detect a gentle whooshing sound, a tickling on the pane, and I acknowledge that my tree is long gone and she is there instead.

There is no time to lose so I send out my message over and over, "I love you, I love you, I love you." I listen to my voice wending out in streams, sprinkling soothing, massaging notes through the air, and I hear it echoed back. "I love you, I love you, I love you."

I carefully lift the grass with a straight-edged shovel and dig at the fibrous earth. I gently pour the ashes from the earthenware pot in amongst the large decaying roots, and I place the grass back on top as best I can, to make it appear undisturbed.

I have returned to sit in the spring sun and sip a cup of tea, but my tea sits untouched on the folding wooden table. A shaft of light catches my eye as it reflects on the outside of my window pane and, without looking down, I remove my sandals. I let my toes wander aimlessly through the grass until they catch on a thick stem. I look to see a poplar shoot growing out of the mended patch of grass. I reach over with my cup of lukewarm tea and gently pour out the potion. It trickles to the earth and seeps downward toward invisible young roots. I do want a guardian to wake me from the night.

Burnt Sienna

❃

RANDALL ELLIOT, RANDY TO HIS FRIENDS, sits in his swivel rocker and stares, with beseeching eyes, at the painting on his wall, as he has done many times before. It is in the style of Cézanne, but the place is not Marseilles Bay; it is a part of Buffalo Lake. Fingers of ultramarine, each created by a single brush stroke, line up to Pelican Point, while raw sienna sand stretches in horizontal lines along the beach. He presumes there are boats tied to the titanium white posts that dot the shore.

Randall closes his eyes and imagines the gentle breeze caressing his sandy hair. He is eight years old and lying flat on his belly on the bow of his father's racing scow. He uses a willow switch, like an artificial limb, to extend his reach and create his own trail in the water. The water slaps a lullaby against the sides of the boat and rocks them both, Randy and Papa, in its lap. They zigzag toward Tony's Island. He can feel the boat moving back and forth as Papa steers with the rudder and swings the boom from side to side.

"Papa, are there animals on Tony's Island?"

"Sometimes the farmer's cattle cross in the winter and get stuck over there."

"No, I mean *wild* animals."

"Maybe some coyotes and rabbits. Probably deer and porcupine. And skunks! We got plenty of skunks."

"No cats?"

"Well, we have been known to have a bobcat around the odd time, and there's always the feral cats that people have abandoned."

"Bobcats! Can we go hunting for bobcats on Tony's Island?"

"We'll see how the weather goes," says Papa as he searches the whole sky for signs of inclement weather.

In the background of the painting, further out in the water, a swirl of indigo and white and cerulean blue work together to reveal turbulence from an unknown source. There is a spot of burnt sienna, like a drop of dried blood, on the water—really a life buoy bobbing near the swirling part of the lake. It is there to save lives.

In the foreground a small boy bends over and digs in the sand with a shovel tinged with titanium white. It is a sunny day. You see his soft cheeks and slanted nose and shaded eyes, all focusing on that jot of sand. A bare-shouldered woman, his mother, sits to the left, facing the water with her back to the artist. Her striped swimsuit curves down into the sand, and you must imagine that her legs are bent in front of her, that her hands are comfortable and relaxed.

Papa, the artist, intends to create a perfect scene. Randy and his mother sit at this particular spot at his father's request.

Randy plans, in his optimistic mind, a castle to rival all sandcastles. It will have towers and turrets and a great moat which he will fill with pails of water from the lake. He will plant a red flag, with a tiger insignia, at the gate. He loves tigers. They will protect his fortress.

His mother seems to spirit herself across the lake. He smells coconut on her oiled skin and sees her mystic smile, but he knows that her eyes, even under dark glasses, take her somewhere across the lake, beyond Tony's Island, somewhere that he has never been.

"Does Tony live on the island?" Randy moves to sit near Papa and shades his eyes with his hand, the one without the willow switch; he has transferred it to his left hand and sometimes holds onto the edge of the boat with his right now that the wind has picked up. Earlier he toyed with sacrificing his switch to the rising waves as a motorboat passed by, but he maintained his grip. After all, he spent a good part of the morning shaving off the bark and nodes with his switchblade.

"Tony used to live in a shack in the middle of the island. But he's dead now."

"Why?"

"He just died, that's all. Lived there alone like a hermit. They say he died in the winter but wasn't discovered until a group of high school boys swam over in the summer and decided to search him out. He built his shack in the middle of the island, screened by poplars and a thicket of wolf willows, so he would be out of sight."

"Can we go see it?"

"Maybe some time." Papa searches the sky again. "There's a storm coming across from Rochon Sands. We'd better head back."

"Ah."

"Another time."

In the evening, when the poplars hiss and the sky rumbles, Randy leans against his mother's side while she reads Rudyard Kipling:

"In the days when everybody started fair, Best Beloved, the Leopard lived in a place called the High Veldt. 'Member it wasn't the Low Veldt, or the Bush Veldt, or the Sour Veldt, but the 'sclusively bare, hot, shiny High Veldt, where there was sand and sandy-coloured rock and 'sclusively tufts of sandy-yellowish grass."

Randy closes his eyes and sees the high Veldt along the northern beach of Tony's Island, and a jungle rises up around Tony's shack. He wants a story about how the tiger got his stripes in the jungle, and his mother tells him he will have to make it up himself.

"Why are they called *Just So* stories?"

"Well, some things just are what they are and there's nothing we can do about it. They are *just so*. There's no other explanation." She gazes across the room the way she sometimes stares across to the far shore of Buffalo Lake. "Besides, Kipling wanted the stories read exactly as he wrote them, just so. You see? Then you sleep so soundly because the words have been said." And she guides him to his bed. She reads more Kipling until he's asleep:

"Let's—oh, anything, Daddy, so long as it's you and me,
And going truly exploring, and not being in till tea!"

Randall still loves tigers and has a collection of tiger prints and drawings in his study, as well as his father's painting. Throughout his adult life Randall has worked for the World Wildlife Fund and has travelled to the ranges and reserves of the Indian and White Indian tigers, the Bengal, Siberian, Sumatran, and even the Caspian and Balinese, though these two are already extinct.

He remains in awe of the tiger. Powerful cats, yet supple and graceful with their killer instinct, they are armed with sharp claws and surgical teeth that can bite through the spinal cord of sizable prey. They gorge on a captured animal while warm blood still courses though its veins, and later, as they guard their lair, they relish the leftovers of putrefied flesh. Still, some are endangered.

Above his desk hangs a framed calligraphic copy of William Blake's *The Tyger*, done especially for him by his mother.

Tyger! Tyger! Burning bright
In the forests of the night,
What immortal hand or eye
Could frame thy fearful symmetry?

Randall closes his eyes again. This time he sees blood dripped onto the white shirt sleeve, first above and then below the burgundy arm band, and dried like burnt sienna. He reviews this scene over and over in his mind. He sees only the back of the shirt. The man sits at his desk with his head turned sideways, his cheek resting on the oak desk top. There is the smell of gunpowder in the air. The man's spectacles are off-kilter with one of the arms sticking up at an odd angle. The clock is *tick-tick-ticking* and something is *drip-dip-dripping*. The inkwell is open and a fountain pen has leaked onto vellum, invading the loops and points of script in the letter, although some words seem to remain clear. He does not, cannot, go too near. Cannot breathe, cannot swallow, cannot speak. Cannot read Papa's story.

Now, with eyes wide open, Randall wants to read his father's letter, but it is too late. Sixty years too late. His mother threw it into the fire where it curled up into carbon confetti and ribbons of smoke, then rose up the chimney into frosty air, like letters to Santa, claiming good behaviour and a wish list of rewards. A lump of coal the colour of red sienna burns in Randall's heart and tightens his chest and stings his eyes so that tears well up. He tries to read the painting because it is all that he has left.

Unrevealed secrets, like hidden putrefied meat, leave a telltale rotten smell, but nothing he can digest. The painting is part of a legacy to his own son, Brian, and sooner or later, probably sooner, it will hang on Brian's wall. Then how will the story go? Just so?

Tattoos

IT CAME IN A DREAM. Arlene would roll her eyes if anyone else said this to her, but there it is. It came in a dream and she responded, bolted out of bed and reacted straight away, impulsive and optimistic. Not her usual self. She stepped into her jeans, pulled on a sweater, and ran her fingers through her hair as she went out the door.

Jenna, who has been gone for over a week, reached out in the night through some sort of mother-daughter ESP and begged her to come. As things are now Arlene has no way to reach the golden-haired Jenna and tell her she is on her way. Mommy is on her way.

"Why," she asks herself, "is the road so vacant today, of all days?" even though she knows the answer. It is too early, just past five in the morning.

Cyclists train along the shoulder lanes as soon as the roads dry up. The locals, in their pickup trucks, take more risks passing the influx of fair-weather drivers. Bikers come out in droves on their Hondas or Harleys to commune in the parking lot at Bragg Creek, some for ice cream, some for dope. But not this morning.

No gas, no cell. Arlene will walk back toward Priddis even if it kills her, hills and all. She has been down this road many times before and has seen a great deal of wildlife—a black bear with her cubs, mule deer, even moose—but never a fox, never a red fox. It raced across the road right in front of her car and continued into the field to her right just before the car coasted to a halt. She has also dodged plenty of roadkill, mostly skunks and deer. Crows signal these deaths from the air before zeroing in on the entrails.

Bonnie Tyler's "It's a Heartache" was on the radio just when Arlene drove past the turn to Priddis, and it seemed so appropriate, resonating in her chest, until Bif Naked came on proclaiming that she loves herself. Now Bif's lines are stuck in her head, in sync with each foot step. Occasionally a magpie interrupts while smaller birds sing a chorus, but otherwise Arlene is totally alone, she thinks.

It is never boring terrain. Going west, from certain hilltops, you can see spectacular vistas of hills and dales, called the High Country, with the backdrop of snow-topped Rocky Mountains. It is thick with spruce and pine. The odd log house nestles deep in the trees, built with the idea of seclusion before the developers arrived. New homes are popping up in parcelled country estates, just down from the private golf course and near the ranches that have spread out for one hundred years or more.

She is closer to someone's house than to the gas pumps at the general store. She could go up the dark tree-lined lane, but who knows what or who is at the end? And she would feel compelled to explain (this is her Achilles heel) why she is out here in the first place, at this time of the morning. So keep walking, she resolves.

Jenna is not missing to everyone. Her friends have assured Arlene that she is in a safe place and just needs a little space. Have faith, don't worry, they all say, but to Arlene this is laughable, though she is mostly in tears.

It started when Jenna and her friend Rachel took the weekend job at The Steak Pit against Arlene's better judgment. Still she drove Jenna to Bragg Creek on a Friday and picked her up from Rachel's on a Sunday afternoon, making it her routine until the disappearance.

It was a long shadowy lane, like the one Arlene has just bypassed. Rachel's mother, Gail, a svelte woman with long auburn hair, maybe ten years younger, would step out in front of their cedar bungalow whenever Arlene arrived for Jenna.

"She'll be out in a few minutes," Gail would advise, always polite but never inviting Arlene inside. Now Gail has disappeared. It is official, not like Jenna's unknown whereabouts. The police have reported Gail missing. Gail's husband, Rachel's stepfather, is missing too.

The truth is that the rift between Arlene and Jenna started before Jenna took that job. It started with tattoos. Okay, it started just before tattoos with the divorce and the strain it put on a young girl to understand the failure of two good parents. Jenna—a sensible girl, they always said—began to immerse herself in the television show *Miami Ink*. She taped it every week and reran episodes featuring her favourite tattoo artist, Kat Von D, who coincidently ran away from home at fifteen. She followed Kat over to *LA Ink* and became obsessed with having a half sleeve portrait, *à la* Kat, tattooed on her arm. Arlene, hoping to dispel the appeal, did some checking and discovered Kat's real name—Katherine von Drachenberg—a name that hinted at respectability if not nobility, as if the formal name would make a difference. In fact it may have kyboshed her intentions. In Arlene's youth jailbirds and addicts and sailors and bikers had tattoos. Now it is respectable, an art form.

A raven glides like some shadow puppet in the forefront of a rising sun. Suddenly there is a ruckus, a cawing and screeching that foreshadows an intruder. "Take another look at me now," she whispers with Bif's voice still rolling through her head. Come to think of it, Bif Naked is covered in tattoos, inked as she transformed herself from Beth to Bif.

Dappled horses commune in a small cluster near the fence. Nearby bushes rustle and a hint of rusty red slips through brush. Arlene walks a little faster, leaves out the rhythm but remembers to take a good last look.

Arlene has tattoos now too. Three of them. Three black dots with a bluish tinge, unlike the hint of brown in any of her moles. They are compass points for her left breast, guides for ionic beams aimed toward rogue cells. Bif Naked probably has these mini tattoos as well as her Egyptian Eye and her various deities. Arlene wonders if the techs could spot them amidst all the other ink.

She has heard that Kat Von D wears the faces and names of a parent, a former husband, and her lovers. Arlene's body, however, is not for display. Her life, thus far, is confidential, though some of it has slipped out for Jenna to see, like glimpses of a fox on a morning drive.

Jenna walked alongside her through the hospital maze as Arlene was wheeled to various places and stages of prep before surgery, intent on supporting her mother. She stood beside Arlene's hospital bed, in the aftermath, but kept her distance just the same. Arlene ached to hold hands, to be hugged as she might have been by a mother or father or husband, if she still had one. Instead Jenna pushed to clear things up, as if she might never have another chance. Why the marriage in the first place? Was it all a sham?

Some avoid the possibility of death. They tiptoe around it, claim it as a rare occurrence, but Jenna faced the prospect head on and revealed an urgent need to define their relationship, to clarify her own life thus far, in case Arlene's was coming to an end. Her persistence was admirable, could even make a mother proud, but Arlene was crushed by the timing.

She has just come over the rise and must stop to claim more air. Her heart pulses in a peculiar way. She waits for it to settle, and then she sees the murder of crows, further along, pecking and scrabbling over something in the ditch. She braces herself to walk by the guts of a fawn or the bloodied fur of a wandering cat. There's no smell of skunk. She usually drives by with windows closed, keeping all scents at bay. It is an unfamiliar odour, putrid, growing stronger with each step.

She covers her mouth and nose with her hand.

At first she sees red, like the tail of the fox she might be trailing. But the tail is going nowhere, tucked in a green garbage bag, a deliberate sign of human folly. She holds her breath. The crows, cocky and belligerent, disregard her as a spoiler, as someone to be feared. They work on an opening further down in the bag and as she sees the target she immediately understands. A hand has worked itself out, pointing painted nails toward the road. And on the wrist is a bracelet of silver-and-blue knots, inked to last a lifetime, allowing verification before becoming a bag of bones.

Arlene runs now, looking for hidden faces along the way. Runs harder than she can ever remember running, even as a child. Runs downhill, off balance, head before feet. No songs play in her head. Just, *oh god, oh god, oh god.*

Her lungs will surely burst. Her senses are so blunted she has not heard the Harley idling in her path.

"Good morning. Are you okay?"

She cannot speak.

"You don't seem the type to be out for a run."

She nods and begins to walk again. Not that she would have a chance in hell to get away.

He adjusts his bandana. "Can I help you?" He sounds exasperated. "Can I give you a ride? Look, I'm a nice guy."

"How would I know?"

He shrugs and then revs his motor.

"Okay. I need to get to Priddis." She is not ready to tell him why.

She has never liked motorcycles—the noise, the dust, the weaving in and out of traffic—yet she clings to his leather jacket like a child to an adored father, partly out of fear and partly resignation. They arrive in the time it would take to brush her teeth; her teeth are clamped tight, her ears are ringing, and her body feels unbendable as though someone will have to pry her off the seat, but somehow she manages to swing her leg over and put both feet on the ground.

"Thanks."

"No problem." He revs the motor but remains in place.

The general store is in darkness, but still she tries to open the door, pulling at it more than once, then peers in through the window. She tries the door again, against all logic, then turns and smiles at her stranger, as though nothing is amiss.

He nods back.

She runs along the boardwalk hoping to see a light in another window, but it is too early. And there isn't a phone booth in sight. She waves at her stranger as if she has accomplished her task but he has turned off the motor and is leaning on his bike, not taken in by her ruse.

"Need any help?" He smiles as if she is an amusement. Cocky like the crows.

"I need a phone."

"Here. Use mine." He pulls his cell out of an inside pocket.

"Okay. Thanks." She now has a rationale. If she calls 911 the RCMP will find her, no matter what. She presses the key pad with her thumb and turns her back for privacy. She knows he is watching but she looks at him again to read off his licence plate for the dispatcher, just in case.

She reveals her message as she hands his cellphone back. "There's a dead body back there." She feels a sudden urge to come clean: to inform and explain and rationalize. She swings from secrecy to a flood of personal babble. "I was going to find my daughter Jenna because I don't know where she is and I ran out of gas and I'm afraid for her and now for me and I am wondering who you really are and … and if you have any tattoos?" The last part tells her how crazy she must sound, how crazy she must be. "Don't answer that."

He no longer seems amused. "You're kidding, right?"

She shakes her head. It occurs to her that he might have family too. Maybe even a daughter. Maybe she is paranoid. "The police are on their way," she says.

The patrol car arrives and as the two men show their badges she feels a wave of guilt and a compulsion to confess. She can explain how the divorce and the cancer and the disagreements may have led to her daughter's split, perhaps all brought on by her own ineptitude. She can admit to impulsively following a dream that led onto this road, before sunrise, with hardly any gas in the car, only to find a dead body. And maybe she has implicated a man because of her anxieties and fears.

She shows her ID and then tells them about her find. Then she waits while her stranger has his turn to talk. She wonders what he is saying. They all look toward her, and she imagines some kind of collusion going on, like in some movie about corrupt cops in an American backwater. Still she is relieved to climb into the back seat of the car and wield control as she guides them to the spot. The Harley follows, apparently free to roam.

She covers her mouth and nose again, and the stranger covers his with his bandana. They check each other's eyes. The police have no choice but to move in closer and call backup and an ambulance, not that the body can be saved. They have put orange pylons on part of the road and staked yellow tape to create a perimeter around the body. She overhears fragments of a call. "Missing ... auburn hair ... wrist tattoo ... foul play."

She has worked it out. "I know who this is," she says but no one seems to hear her. She raises her voice. "Excuse me. I think I know who this is." But it does not seem a mystery to anyone, not the police or the stranger or the crows who watch from the branches of skeletal poplars.

"They know who it is," the stranger says, his calm contrasting with her panic.

New fears form in her mind. "We have to find my daughter," she cries.

"We'll get to you," says an officer with barely a look in her direction. Traffic is beginning to pass in the remaining single lane, and people are staring like scavengers of doom.

Arlene finally has the chance to explain that her daughter,

Jenna, is a friend of Rachel, who is most likely the daughter of the woman now lying in the ditch. A dispatch is sent to Bragg Creek requesting the girls' location.

Arlene is in tears when a leather arm embraces and consoles her. She offers no resistance.

"I have two," he says.

"What?"

"Tattoos."

She looks up, embarrassed.

He takes off his jacket and begins to pull off his shirt.

"Oh, please don't," she says.

"See, I have these hearts, one above the other, looking to embrace."

The hearts lay sideways, the points facing opposite directions and forming tails that curve round toward each other.

"And this is a wandering bear."

He has a tattoo on each upper arm, all in black. Not half sleeves but they stretch over his biceps just the same. They are nicely done, she thinks.

"I'm sorry." She begins to apologize but is interrupted.

"Okay Brent, could you help this lady get some gas?" It is obvious that Brent is no stranger to the police, and now, for her, he has a name. He pulls his shirt back on and slides into his jacket.

Arlene is on the road again, listening to Nirvana on the radio. Something draws her in. It's inexplicable—her and Kurt Cobain. Jenna is back in school and has admitted to Arlene that her life is not so bad, especially when she considers Rachel's plight. Arlene has allowed that tattoos are not so bad either. Rachel's mother, Gail, is gone forever. Arlene is still here, out for a drive on the same road that Gail's body was dumped.

The leaves of the poplars and willows have unfurled, though they are still the size of pennies, and the hills are in variegated shades of green. Kurt is also gone forever, but his voice is still on air as she reaches the crest of the steepest hill and stops to take in the rolling land and peaked mountains. She turns off the ignition but still hears his voice over and over and over in her head. She can't decide if his lyrics are simple-minded, drug-addled or profound, or maybe all three, but she agrees, this *is* all we are. She wonders what inks and designs he chose to have injected into his skin. And she wonders if Brent will happen along on his Harley.

Acknowledgements

Thank you to my fellow writers Lori Hahnel, Betty Jane Hegerat, and Astrid Blodgett for their advice and encouragement. Thank you to all the small literary magazines, be they print or online, for providing a venue for short story writers. Thank you to Inanna Publications for valuing a woman's point of view, and to Luciana Ricciutelli for her editing skills. And thank you to old acquaintances and new for just being you, and sometimes revealing a germ of a story.

"Burnt Sienna." *Pottersfield Portfolio* 22.3 (2003). Winner, Compact Fiction Contest, Winter/Spring 2003.

"Flight 2100." *The Windsor Review* 39. 2 (April 2007).

"Gourmet Cooking." *The Broken City* 12 (Summer 2013). Web.

"Hair Matters." *The Steel Chisel* (November 2014). Web.

"Here's Looking at You." *Turk's Head Review* (Winter 2013). Web.

"Life in Cars." *FreeFall* 24.3 (Fall 2014).

"Lila." *The Nashwaak Review* 28/29.1 (Summer/Fall 2012).

"Marrying Stationery." *The Toronto Quarterly* 6 (2010).

"No Regrets." *Frostwriting* 6 (April 2011). Web.

"Rockin' Around the Royal Bank of Canada." *Qwerty* 26 (Spring 2011).

"Rosemary." *Turk's Head Review* (November 2015). Web.

"Shifting." *Raven Chronicles* 17.1-2 (Spring/Summer 2012).

"Silvia." *Words, Pauses, Noises* (December 7, 2014). Web.

"Special Occasions." *The Nashwaak Review* 26/27.1 (Summer/Fall 2011).

"Svea." *Femmuary* (February 2016). Web.

"Tattoos." *The Nashwaak Review* 34/35 (Summer/Fall 2015).

"The Guardian." *Room of One's Own* 17.3 (September 1994).

"Transforming Doctor Zhivago." *The Antigonish Review*, 163 (Fall 2010).

Photo : Neil Speers Photography

Barbara Biles is a Calgary writer. She attended the University of Alberta and taught primary school until her own daughter and son were born. She explored fiction writing in extension courses and local writing groups. Her short fiction has appeared in Canada, the U.S, the UK, and Sweden, in various literary magazines including, *FreeFall, The Nashwaak Review, The Antigonish Review, The Windsor Review,The Broken City, Turk's Head Review, Femmuary* and others. *Dear Hearts* is her debut collection of short fiction.